EVERYDAY STORIES

MIMA MIHAJLOVIĆ

EVERYDAY STORIES

told by Mima Mihajlović, an observer with a wide range of interests

Translated from the Bosnian by Filip Paštrović and Žana Arnautović

Edited by Maria Badanova and Ivanka Čizmić

Illustrations by Elvis Dolić/Doliccommics

© 2021, Mima Mihajlović

Afterword © 2021, Medina Džanbegović

Publishers Maxim Hodak & Max Mendor

Interior design by Max Mendor

© 2021, Glagoslav Publications

www.glagoslav.com

ISBN: 978-1-912894-34-5

First published in English
by Glagoslav Publications in May 2021

EVERYDAY STORIES

MIMA MIHAJLOVIĆ

Translated from the Bosnian
by Filip Paštrović and Žana Arnautović

GLAGOSLAV PUBLICATIONS

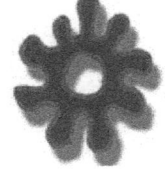

Contents

"Boredom is endless," Titoslav thought and lit a third cigarette.

It should have been the last one of the day, since it was the thousandth time he had "definitely" stopped smoking.

He was sitting in his favorite café, trying to figure out what the hook-nosed moron was telling the caked-up blonde, whose face wasn't visible under the three tons of makeup, which, of course, didn't match her wardrobe.

"Those women are really silly," he thought. "They probably get up at 5 a.m. to put all that makeup on so that at 7 a.m. they are battle-ready."

He imagined how that blonde looked in the morning when she woke up. She would certainly have black circles under her eyes because she took the makeup off too quickly.

Can you imagine the shock of waking up next to a zombie after you went to bed with a sex-bomb (thought hook-nose)?

Outside it started raining. What bullshit! His jeans would get dirty up to his ass again, and he had just taken them off the drying rack this morning. What is that God thinking?! Probably has a bladder infection!

"I hate rain!" he said out loud. He probably wouldn't have noticed it unless the blonde and hook-nose had turned around and looked at him questionably. Why did they have to sit at this table?! Couldn't they have barged onto some other table? When he looked around and saw that all of the tables were taken, he thought they should have gone somewhere else to chirp.

BLOND ON BLONDE
ŠKOLA
SEX
JUNE
Cool 18
BANG
Satisfaction
EVERYDAY
STORIES

The music was dreadful. The waiter, who happened to be a minor, was playing some mega-turbo-super cocktail songs which he was obviously enjoying. How he had just slammed the coffee on the table! To him! Ah, he is new, so he still doesn't know.

Ah, Sejo, a businessman, employs all kind of brats. But fuck that! Sejo is the only one from the whole generation who has made any real money. But also a lot of enemies. Ah, Sejo is a good guy, he does what he does best. School was never his thing anyway. He was always talking about how he would become the Boss. And he made his dream come true.

He used to turn his hand to singing, as well. Their first school band wasn't bad. They could have made something of it if Sejo hadn't snatched Melita, Muha's girlfriend, while he was in the army.

Melita got her cherry popped at Sejo's weekend house, while the January snow was falling. The rest of the gang, who were dead drunk, were making a snowman in front of the weekend house. And Muha, freezing on guard duty in some shithole, was daydreaming how he would write a ballad for Melita once he came home. Better than Brega's "Lullaby."

No one could drink on the tab in Sejo's bar, only Titoslav was allowed to, who knows why. Sejo probably knew that he couldn't be at war with the whole world, and Tisi was some sort of connection to the past, to those times when everybody had the same dreams, replaying "Satisfaction" for the millionth time and arguing who the better poet was, Jimmy or Bob. There, just when he thought his life wandering was over, when, fuck, his little chick dumped him.

Girls are cool until they turn eighteen. After that, they think too much. They don't unreservedly suck up your nebulous story, they don't admire your sexy ass anymore, and they don't find it great that you are a little bit older.

It's okay as long as it ends that way. But if they realize they're "nice girls" who are some class above you, they can't allow that, all the family members from the intermediate to extended family start asking:

"Who is that hippie? Sanja, darling, is he using drugs?"

You, of course, spit on that small town jabber, but your little girl has already cracked under the pressure. Chicks from your generation are quite a problem, too! They are completely in a mindset that if they gave you pussy, marriage is just around the corner, and the ones that are a bit more liberal don't want to grope in the parks anymore. They want a guy with a car who shops in Trieste or at least an empty place where you could bang properly.

Well, but that's Sejo's area. Although his wife keeps him on a short leash, so if he does snatch something on the side, it's in secret.

He really thought he had everything under control. He thought the girl had really snapped, and when the end of school came and she passed the entrance exam for the college of dentistry in a far-away town, she told him in a sorrowful voice that it would be best if they broke up because she didn't believe in long-distance love.

Ah, bullshit, love! A province girl got hooked on the big city, student life, new people, and the new gig! And now what?! There were fewer and fewer chicks (at least the ones that got turned on by hollow philosophical masturbation and ideal horoscope matches), and Tisi was 28 years old and had a good working record as a train dispatcher. And an eternal boy…

II

T. abruptly got out of bed, drenched in sweat. It took him a couple of seconds to come to his senses and look at the clock. Four o'clock in the morning.

This really was a fucking nightmare!

He had dreamt that guards in a madhouse were choking him in front of a mirror, and he couldn't erase the image from his consciousness, the image of his deformed face.

III

"Baby, stop playing with me! I know really well what you actually want!"
"Leave me alone, you drunk idiot, you are disgusting!"

***

Music raised him from the dead for the millionth time.

Who gave a crap if the boss had met a friend from the past, Leila was late for the bus, Predo was back on heroin again, and mom had cancer. He wasn't even thinking of the mirror anymore.

Only Dandy was still harassing him. Nothing helped against him. Not even flipping movies, music, nor alcohol, nor sedatives.

Hopefully it won't go sideways again. Oh God! Again with the gibberish! He is not up for it! He is too alive! Boban told him long ago that he is not what he used to be. The only thing that was keeping him in his decadent deal was his hair. Although it cracked up halfway up the head (especially in the

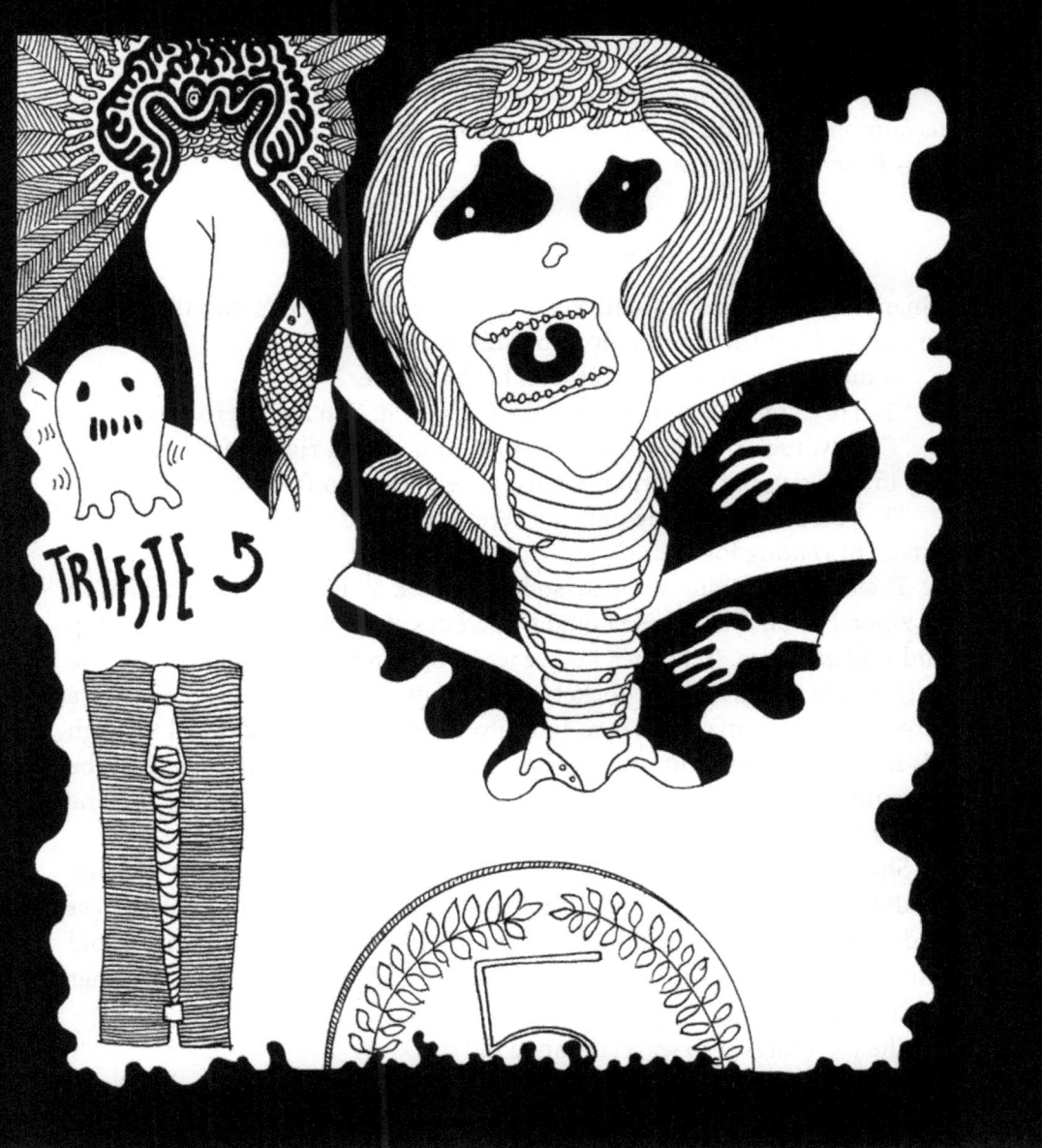

back), still, there were no signals of baldness, even though he would lose 75 hairs after every washing (he counted them). And for that chick, he washed it twice a week. God, where had she taken him?! He hated her! Because of her nose. He hated her!

Dandy again. Like a scarecrow behind the curtains with the same story all the time:

– *It is not the one who knows the truth and speaks it that is right, but the one who holds his lie for the truth!* (M.P. writer)

– Yuck! The Arts Academy in Sarajevo is not as clean as it seems. It washes its hair once a month. Think how many hairs fall off then!
– Born to be wild! (4 ever)

IV

"Snap those fingers, snap 'em! If you continue like that, in a month you will end up without them. Who do you think you are?"

"A moron in a straightjacket with his hands free."

"You're diluted. You don't have the balls for it. You are a zero, man!"

"Dandy, fuck off! You know, just as I do, who is right here. Stay here, day in, day out, but you still remain a ghost, and I don't believe in ghosts."

"T., you are completely out of it. Weaker by the minute, though I have time. I'm waiting for you…"

The rain had finally stopped, so he could be on his way. It got colder, so he zipped up all the way. He bought cigarettes at Auntie Mary's corner shop and walked home. In his head there was a buzzing, he was shaking, and he put his cold hands into his pockets. At the bottom of his left pocket, he felt a forgotten coin from somewhere and automatically started flicking it through his fingers. He concentrated on that small, yellow coin. And just then, he encountered his high school teacher. So, like any other well-trained dog, he pulled his hands out of his pockets to greet her.

She went on like a wound up toy! About how terribly sorry she was that he didn't go to college. How he'd killed it in physics class, how she'd never had a student like him, and some other crap. It's like she lives in some stupid American movie. His dad is not a "Rockefeller"! His dad is like any other "father" in this fucking city, a failed drunk with failed ideas.

She took forever to leave, damned old bag.

The wind was blowing so intensely that he thought his ears would fall off. Ah, who cares about the ears, save the eyes, they are still the most important.

***

The morning decides the entire day.

Which means the day will be crappy. It's the way it is. The more you sleep, the sleepier you become.

You wake up in the morning with a swollen head, with a primordial thirst, and a burned up throat. And there is a buzzing in your brain:

Just let me get to the bathroom in time, so I don't piss myself.

"I should go somewhere… It got too stuffy in here. The air is so heavy that one can't take it anymore. And where on Earth should I go?! And with whom? Ah, she really got rid of me!"

Titoslav was one of those men who didn't care who they hit on. Wherever he found himself, he was constantly in between younger girls, searching for some undiscovered love of his life. He would pull every trick in the book and some killer smile or some move, and by some miracle, women loved him. But only for the first month. Tisi was completely and hopelessly trapped in the past, and he was amazed by the ones who weren't. He was hopelessly falling in love, enjoying his masochistic Goethe's acts on a daily basis. It was enough that a girl looked at him with a bit of interest, and he was done.

But Dandy spoke again:

"T., you are a sick person. No, you were born sick. Your mother carried you in her womb all mangy and rotten already. That's why she became ugly during her pregnancy. As if she was, even then, carrying a cancer cell in her body, not you! T., you are like the scabies, and whatever you touch, you cover that in scabs. You were born to be eaten by maggots! And for them to start doing that ahead of time, around your thirties. When everyone is at the peak of their life, you are already dead. You're dead! And such a pathetic masochist like you actually wants that."

Titoslav jerked as if somebody had given him an evil eye. But he said nothing. No, in five seconds he was already screaming, as if he was being butchered!

No, he just looked speechlessly into an imaginary dot.

No, cramping up from pain and screaming.

No! Still looking at the dot.

No, no! Screaming and cramping up inside of himself, but in reality, he was quiet and speechlessly looking into the same imaginary dot.

V

Why don't humans, on the day of their birth, have their fate written on the sky?

Because God made sure that the Earth has loafers and failed philosophy students. For Tisi, it was clear from the beginning. But like Dandy explained it nicely, a straightjacket with your hands free is a nice thought, and as each nice thought, it was practically unfeasible.

Titoslav's obsession was making flowers out of paper. He was very conscientious in that useless ritual, even managing to force the people around him, even if they didn't join him, to at least stare blindly at that stupid ceremony. Those flowers most often ended up in a flowerpot and often under the table.

***

They were stripping down slowly, in the rhythm of the music. They had put down the green blinds, so they didn't have to look at each other. Their intercourse was based on touches, not stares. There, another controversy! Although the eyes are the most important part of a person, with her, they were not needed. Stares brought down the general mood. Therefore, they were stripping in the rhythm of the music. They didn't see each other, nor were they touching, each were in their own corner; so that was pretty much it. Coming closer was not slow, like the stripping (which, to put it lightly, was full of fear), because the mood had reached a peak level of stress.

The binding was almost painful. It usually ended with her blubbering, that came from the bottom of her guts, which was followed by her getting cold feet. He would then put them in between his, and they would stay like that for a couple of minutes. In those moments, when it was all said and done, T. had no idea what to say. That was his tiny handicap in a way, because he knew chicks loved big words.

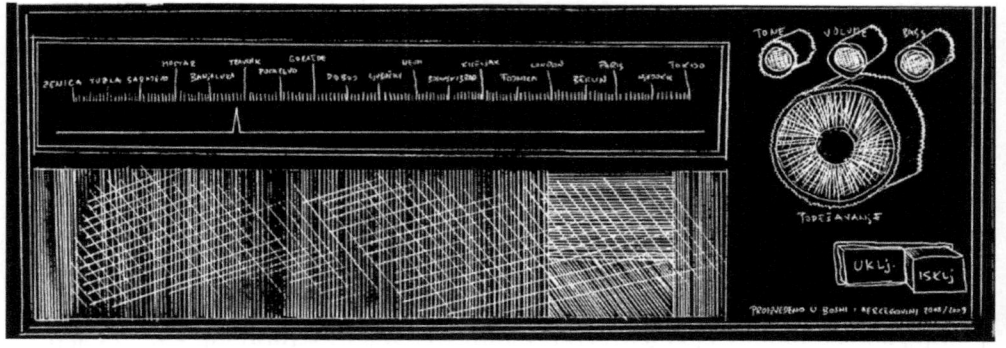

14

RABIT
see
B. O.

VI. The Rabbit Hunt

The last few days Titoslav had done a lot of running in the rain, because, as usual, he was late for work. The boss was infuriated! He would usually throw car keys at him, or the glasses pouch. And he used to be a lot worse! For example, it's New Year's Eve – why should you be hungover at work, when you can just stay at home in bed? He doesn't give a damn about all the trains of this world. Plus, his train left a long time ago. You simply lie in bed, pull the blanket up to your chin, and enjoy.

T. hated Sundays. It didn't matter if it was sunny or not. Although he was done with school a long time ago, he still had the feeling (like an atavism) of the hollow Sunday because of fucking Monday. In fact, Sunday was a silent capitulation of freedom. He was usually sitting at home the whole day, listening to music, putting together flowers made out of paper, pretending he didn't hear his dad, throwing up in the bathroom the whole morning, and mom coincidentally making a racket with the plates.

All the songs and albums that used to put him in a certain mood had no effect anymore, and there wasn't a place to get new ones. T. was absolutely ruthless when it came to newspapers. Days were passing, and he could feel his creativity slowly fading.

"I'll end up becoming a stone sleeping man," he had the tendency to say.

One day he got the idea to put on suit pants and shoes with "acorns" and socks, Michael Jackson style. But he gave up quickly, as he had none of the abovementioned things. He only could have taken the olive-green tie from his dad, since each military person had to have one.

Whenever he put on a tie to go with a shirt from his collection of plaid ones, he would end up looking like a retarded youngster from a gymnasium basement.

"These commercials on the radio are completely destructive, I really don't know who buys something after such a stupid message."

"I don't know, my son, but believe me, Ševala lost fifteen kilos with those teas," his mom said.

"Mom, you've also gone out of your mind!"

Dandy hid behind the curtain and started singing:

"Bunny runs from afar
covered in sweat
The poor bunny runs, thirsty, hungry, and sighs "Ah"
He's gotten frightened, because someone yelled out "Stop"
Stop, bunny stop, and tell me
do you shed
Because there's a dog
that bit a cook
the cook took a knife
and tore him whole.
Blood to his knees (Panonian Satan would have cum already)
tense like a motherfucker."

***

T. and B., friends from childhood, decided one summer (somewhere at the end of the school year 1981/82) that they would go to Peru, no more, no less. Somewhere, in some book, they had read about the beauties of South America. They were delighted by the small smiling people and decided to experience that for themselves.

As you can tell by this story, they ended up at the Austrian border, but they had a good time nevertheless. On the return trip, in Maribor, they hooked up with two young Slovenian girls, who were completely free and ready for fun.

16

They blasted down to Pula, where they slept on benches and stole water-melons. They drank the cheapest wine and laughed endlessly. They swam during the night, sang, screamed, and knocked down newspaper stands. Somewhere around the fourth day, the cops took away the two girls because their parents had been looking for them all over the country. The police questioned the two fellas, wrote them up, gave them a few slaps on the cheek and, by some miracle, released them. They were running around Pula's streets for another day, after which they stole a wallet from a rich German, got two tickets to Makarska, met up with some people they met at a concert, and ended up being in their camp for a while...

As Djoka would say, "It's all Tom Sawyer's fault."

Dandy again:

"You again T., you are again in the past! That story is a decade old and you regularly retell it to every pussy, like it's some adventure movie!"

"Dandy, it was really good, back in those days, you know that too!"

"Tisi, if you weren't so pathetic, you would be comical."

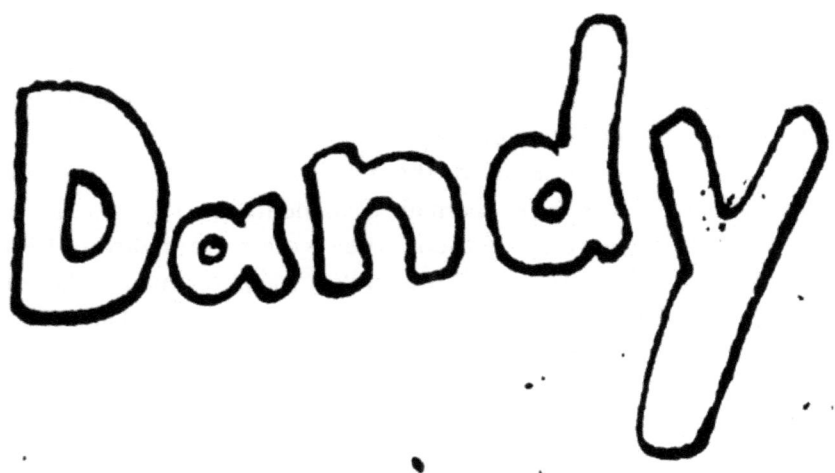

Dandy

To have a bit of an overview of this story, Dandy gets a big introduction in this title. T. and Dandy are actually one unbreakable symbiotic unity, but in this case – two parasites who alternate the roles.

Some friends of T. claim that Dandy appeared in T.'s life on one sad day, when our main character got his first undeserved slap from his drunk father, and his mother shoved his first Prozac down his throat, because T.'s mother, in her kind primitive head, didn't know how to calm down the hysterical crying of a surprised child.

Actually, then, T. opened the door to Dandy and let him into his life.

The writer of this story knows from reliable sources that Dandy and T. have been living together since the beginning. But, like we all know, a parasite can be in hibernation for years before it gets the appropriate moment to appear. Dandy was fearless. Nothing and nobody could stop him except, of course, Fear.

Fear

We can't notice it in this story, because you can't grab it by its head or tail. Just when we think we recognized it, it changes its shape, taking a completely new form, but it's always around. Like every constant of this world, FEAR is eternal. That's why games with it are fucked.

VII

Despite overwhelming avoidance, Fear and Dandy met each other one evening. Fear jumped on Dandy's back and tried to choke him. And it almost succeeded! After a while, when Dandy finally found courage, he suggested to Fear to play an open card game. With the stakes being T. (of course, Fear recommended it).

At the beginning, Dandy couldn't accept a game with that kind of stakes. I hope you see the reasons were obvious. Everything was at stake.

Fear decided to use frontal attacks (which was very strange because Fear was usually accustomed to guerrilla warfare), something that it uses rarely, i.e., only when it wants something for its benefit.

Dandy thought his defense was shallow and crazy, only realizing afterwards that it was the only correct thing that he had ever done. Despite his limbs shaking insanely and the hunger threatening to take astronomical proportions, Dandy couldn't stop himself. Fear was injecting some disgusting, stinking fluid into his brain, and at that moment it was completely paralyzing him.

No matter how much stronger Fear was, using its insidious warfare, Dandy had some sort of advantage. He was someone who had nothing to lose because he knew from the very beginning that his victory was temporary, and the victory of Fear was eternal.

As there were time constraints, for some stupid technical reason, Fear and Dandy stopped their war, game, or clash, till the next story.

"I wanna go home!!!!!!!"

Titoslav woke up again from his own words, somewhere between two everyday thoughts. For a moment, he thought how home was nothing but the conformity of a closed type, where you put Freedom in an expensive, golden frame.

IX

In his free time, and T. had plenty of time (because of some small "technical issues" which were killing his ambition to start doing something that brings happiness, something smart and profitable), he was on the question of fake morals. He explained it during a rush of rich words:

Escape from additional obligations,
Conformity of the closed type!

The fear of a taboo theme, caused by brainwashing since childhood and so on, shyness from identity. He often imagined the world without that useless barrier, but it was hard, because T., just like any other human, was a hypocrite. He realized that if he wanted to leave this vicious circle, he only had to wait, since the same thing seen at two different moments doesn't look the same at all.

His favorite subject for endless philosophizing was also daydreaming. He could think of a whole movie with himself as the main character and enjoy, for hours, that mix of thrill and fear, excitement and erection, drunkenness and who knows what else. Those were not the goodness of ordinary moments, not in any case; those were surrogates of a human's life, unfulfilled in reality. Daydreaming brings satisfaction in oneself to every human being. And daydreams never leave a bitter aftertaste or regret. That gives them endless security in regards to reality.

Clothes

Clothes are a function for the body, but what is a body to clothes? It's what you put on when you are cold or what you take off when you are warm. Clothes are the things you like to put on or take off. It's the thing that wakes desire or the thing that irritates you when you have to pull the underwear out of your ass each time you stand up. It's the thing you hate to iron, fold, or wash.

In any case, you could write a whole story about such a simple thing, but the characteristics of us, i.e. people, are that we complicate and completely exaggerate simple things, and thus we overload our brains and are not capable anymore to separate the important from the unimportant. Which means that we have completely forgotten that the main point of clothes was exclusively thermal.

And now it's cosmic.

***

Tisi slowly got out of bed and went to the bathroom. Mechanically grabbing the toothbrush, he started brushing. In the beginning fast, then slower and slower. From a distance he could hear the radio playing in the kitchen, again news full of tension, for a moment getting scared by what he heard, but then forgetting it quickly. How he hated to bathe. It wasn't always like that, only in these last couple of years, because there is always something missing. Either there is no water or electricity or shampoo, or there is no water and electricity, and so it goes in circles until you go through all the possible combinations.

In fact, everything was falling apart little by little, and he was pretending, like the rest of the little people, that it wasn't his business. What does it matter if inflation is 100% a day or that he didn't get his paycheck for 3 months, but instead some coupons, or that everyone is waiting in line every morning for brown bread (because the price for white bread has risen a whopping 400%) and mom doesn't like to waste a single gram of flour (saving it for the bad days, like they haven't already come).

He was back to his thoughts in the bathroom. While he was dressing, he thought how lucky he was to be a man. Imagine all that waxing, periods, hair styling, fucking about. When every morning before school his sister gets in the bathroom before him, she stays in there for a century. It feels, for the thousandth time, like he gives away all the positive things about being a woman (during puberty he had a phase of curiosity about what it's like to be a woman).

Looking at the sock drawer, he realized he didn't have a matching pair. An everlasting problem. He should go to Muha. He needs an audience again and a shoulder to cry on, which means Muha will sit down and listen. And listen. And listen. And he is not going to nod his head or give any comments. At the end of the monologue, Muha is only going to look at him with his angelic, half drunken eyes. And then it's done. Because Tisi is completely incompetent of dialogue. Having a discussion with him was like an assault on windmills. He used the power of appearance, being very virtuous in wordplay. All in all, he was completely subjective.

The monologue at Muha's place ended as usual. Tisi went home with the weight off his mind, still with uncertainty and small differentiation of a man who had an inferiority complex.

***

Dandy reported again. He wasn't around for 3 days. Just then, T. was at the peak of his everlasting insecurity, and Dandy was the last thing he needed.

"Have you seen those workers?"

"Which workers?!"

"That gray mass of faces, they were all passing through you and beside you when you were coming back from work. It isn't possible that you haven't noticed them. They all had your face and they were all thinking the same as you. And they all had the same thing waiting for them at home, just like you, that's why no one was in a hurry."

The biggest insult you could have told Tisi had just been spoken. He had such a pubescent hard-on for originality, that it was tragicomic! He pouted like a tiny dog to Dandy's words, defending himself stubbornly.

"Ha, ha, ha, ha…" Dandy laughed, and for the first time he didn't feel any satisfaction but some sheer empathy and some emptiness in his stomach.

X

Like I said, Dandy wasn't feeling anything.

Then a long period of anxiety came. It was caused by external events that were very familiar to us.

Those "middle" moods were killing him. He was a prisoner and had an irresistible urge to scream. He was horrified by those primitive minds, who overnight turned into Satan's followers, passionately waving flags, singing false hymns like barbarians and sharing between themselves something that belonged only to God.

A phase of exaggerated existence in a period of overcoming was so familiar, thought Titoslav, packing a so-called "bug-out bag" with contents that had been standard for decades: documents, a few family photos, cans, some basic clothing, and a sentimental object.

A luxury version of that would, eventually, contain a little battery-powered radio with a spare pair of batteries, a first aid kit that you would find in a car, and chocolate.

"T., I came to tell you, stay strong buddy! I'm just an old guy and a damned dickhead. Better to be a fool than spinning in a circle..."

An old memory went through T.'s head. It was after the Olympics, I think. The early summer morning was chilly. Who could think that the asphalt would get glowing hot at noon?! It smelled of love, the river, and smog.

When he appeared on the platform, Bobby wasn't there yet. He checked his watch: 6:08 a.m., Sunday. He told his old man everything right to his face a day ago. Mom was crying and begging him to stay. He pulled it off pretty theatrically! His brother just looked at him and laughed, while his sister said:

"Hey philosopher, you promised to help me with tomorrow's essay! See you, I'm in a rush!" and ran out of the house happily.

He put some nonsense into the backpack: the unavoidable sleeping bag and a few books. That night he was again dreaming of how the guards were choking him in front of the mirror. In the morning, his desire to leave was even greater. Although it was chilly, he sat in the garden of the station's café.

6:18 a.m. No sign of Bobby

6:23 a.m.

6:42 a.m. Still not there

He was cold. And the chair started to be uncomfortable. He thought that he would end up with hieroglyphs embedded on his ass, when he gets up. He jumped at the announcer's voice:

"*The fast train number 849 from Kardeljevo through Mostar, Sarajevo, Zenica, Doboj, Vinkovci, Zagreb, Ljubljana and Munich for Stuttgart is coming to the third track... The passengers are asked to have their documents ready, and the passengers with reservations please step forward to the first wagon. For all our local alcoholics, there is our overpriced buffet at your disposal and our customs agents will make sure to harass you as much as possible, unless you are a young divorcee, so make sure you spread your legs a little bit in order to transfer your illegal bags over the border with ease... All small-time thugs are asked to check their IDs to see if they at least a little bit resemble the guy in the photo in the stolen passport. And for our guest workers, there is not only the buffet, but also non-stop radio at your disposal: Mega-Turbo folk hits from your homeland... We wish you safe travels. Ah yes, one more thing. The fast train number 849 from Kardeljevo to Stuttgart is actually 186 minutes late, which means you can rest at ease and be bored, because stressing out is not worth it."*

All of a sudden Tile saw Bobby, who was running across the rails like a maniac.

No, not fast and full of fucking confidence, but walking slowly towards him.

No! He looked bewildered, with hangdog eyes, a real cowardly pussy one, and he was breathing with a half-open, wet mouth.

NO! NO! NO!

He is not going!!!

The end. And it hasn't even started yet.

It was a sign of an everlasting capitulation of one's youth, and so little was needed, so little...

XI

Dandy didn't know how to climb those fucking stairs. Constantly tripping over his own trouser leggings or some fucking stone, there for who knows what reason. He was asking himself for the thousandth time if he could do anything and still remain a human, or at least what's left of him, when he loses everything, left only with little hope and everlasting fear, especially when you know that the nearer future is in the hands of Satan's followers.

Actually, this waiting was like some liminal state or that terribly annoying dream that you have before dawn, when the majority of people dream some rubbish. When you have one of those stupid fevers, 37.5 C, when all you want to do is roll around in bed and overeat.

He thought he was going to be engaged from one side or another from the very beginning. The scared, the pissed off, and those with complexes had already been involved.

Ah, it's really hard to stay smart and choose the lesser evil.

And it still is.

Little Story

"I am going. And you know that it's time, everyone goes their own way."

"I know and I say I HATE! Because I can't do anything. And I'm afraid."

When he at last returned after so many months of hell, he didn't know how to tell her.

And he knew he had to. He thought how good it was where things were black and white and how some things wouldn't be clear to him if it wasn't so. It seemed that only in Hell he'd accepted his almost sick love for her.

When he saw her after such a long time, all his dreams reached their peak and only roughness remained. And body. He wanted her right there, in the middle of the street. He wanted for them to cry together, to scream.

"I want to tell you because it hurts. The past and future hurt terribly. And I can't escape them. I can't!"

"Sometimes it seems to me that life is a mild intoxication, neither in the sky nor on the earth, and I want to love you, right now!"

"It looks like we've changed roles. Or haven't we? My dear, you have no idea what's happening, and what's worse, you will soon find out, and I can't protect you. I don't understand how it is that we've grown up overnight, and how entirely different things matter now. Everything is even somewhat nice because it's so simple. But not the time… not…"

A soldier, centuries-old constant, is none other than a fucking Hasan-aga, as someone once put it so nicely a long time ago. And we're all in shit, up to the neck…

My Little Girl used to say that we love only once and usually tragically, and the rest are just surrogates of that first, tragic love. Personally, I never agreed with that. My Little Girl had always been a little pathetic anyway.

"And I say again… there is no more God… until the next moment…"

***

At the beginning there was one little Zero, who had no idea who she was or what she was or where she was. A classic identity crisis, such a familiar thing in this region! As time passed, she got used to physiological needs and, who knows why, she often came into conflict with the time she lived in.

Instincts were still undeveloped, and it was just a matter of time when they would come to the surface.

There, it was like that at the beginning.

At the beginning of every suffocation of primary freedom, Dandy was surprised. No, he wasn't angry, not at first. He was just scared and very, very sad at the beginning. And everything was so simple. There were only two decisions, colors or rights, call it whatever you want.

Secondary freedom is something else. It consists of a thousand little, tiny things that make up life. In this phase, instincts have already been awoken, the laws of the strongest have largely been established, and there is no place for objectivity here.

XII

As a child, T. had had his own world, something like Alice or Dorothy. He loved kicking the ball far, farther than his gaze could reach. He was no revolutionary. T. had been the classical example of a rebel, entirely unaware of his surroundings, though his surroundings were aware of him.

He'd been fascinated by animals and had always brought home all kinds of jars with frogs, insects, wounded birds, abandoned dogs and cats. He would sit for hours in front of his jars staring at those creatures. There was a slight jubilation because of his control over them, disgust, and astonishment. He would grimace and stick out his tongue, and when he accidentally saw his reflection in the mirror with unknown eyes, he would wonder, and was ashamed.

He was dreaming infinitely. Usually of some deep and heavy water full of sharks and swimmers. In those dreams, he would normally be on a sailing plank or a rubber boat, with half of his body in the water, rowing with his arms in a panic toward that black and white vastness, and only some crazy luck, in the midst of waking, would save him from the sea monster at the last moment.

In one of his countless séances in front of the mirror, he felt something, like a touch or a gentle stroke on his head (only after many years, when it happened again, he began believing in the lost souls who appear that way in this world).

He realized that no part of the human body is symmetrical. His left eye was more open, more piercing, and his left eyebrow was always reproachfully higher. His left cheek had always had more pimples than the right, and the left part of his forehead was always covered with a thicker strand of hair.

On the other side, the right eye was somehow more passive, calmer, maybe even drunk or wounded.

T. was a crazy. Perhaps even too bitter and melancholic. Only after those, let's call them "good," times passed would he become aware of them. He often thought that maybe he should've been beaten then, to wake up and enjoy them while they lasted.

But screw the man who is satisfied with the "retired life" and to whom, in his crucial years, everything is just enough. He'd wanted so much, strongly and passionately, but pushiness and ambition weren't his stronger qualities, and that had cost him quite a bit in his later life.

XIII

At dawn the sun spread over the clouds and was barely shining over the charred earth. Drunken soldiers were spread out all around the camp. Usually they snored loudly and sporadically, occasionally scratching their hairy bellies or pushing their dirty, swollen hands into their pants. A muted song could be heard from the half-demolished barrack. It was more like a cry, a lullaby, or a calling. It was a song without words.

Hasan-aga opens his eyes with ease, then immediately covers them again with his hands, because some lost ray of light has managed to get in through the broken glass and hit him right in the eye. He felt a light and slow pain and didn't remember anything. In the distance nothing could be heard.

"Good," he thought. "It seems even this jungle sometimes rests."

He loved these two seconds of each morning the most, those empty seconds without feeling and reminiscence. Afterwards, everything is different. Pictures line up one after the other, harder and stronger, and there is no return.

He realized he was sick and that he had to throw up urgently. If he had gone to the window a second later, he would have barfed the contents of his stomach right onto the head of the one on the bed. Huh! He was filled with something between disgust and bliss. He took a deep breath of sharp, morning air and straightened.

Everything is great. He doesn't have a nightmare. He's usually troubled by daytime ones, so he can defend himself out of trouble by means of daily activities. Perhaps it's because of those colorful friends who make that co-matose, dreamless sleep possible.

He washed up his face quickly. Water dripped on the yellow sink and like an eel ran somewhere.

"Like blood," he thought. His brain was screaming.

"I don't want to think, I don't want to think, I mustn't think, but then… I want to fuck her, I want to love her, to hold and hug her!" he was roaring within. "God, if you are there, let me wait it out, even if it's just for one day!"

"Paranoid idiot! How foolishly he'd stepped on that mine. Coward…"

He was used to it now. He'd found justification in the mass hysteria and total blindness, which had finally overtaken his primordial chill, and every-thing was somehow easier.

"Crash, burn, saw, shoot, break, tie, and hijack in the name of… There was once a conformity of the closed type…"

Sometimes he thought: "*Why do we, people, hate each other so much and how haven't we become tired of it through all these centuries?*" And how is our entire civilization nothing but a heap of wars or the periods between two wars, where we are thinking up a better, bigger, and technically more perfect slaughter. And we have called that history. If we are not alone in this universe, then the aliens are probably ashamed in our name and are wondering how they could've happened to be in the same solar system as such primitives.

So, it is not surprising that no one wants to hang out with us. For a few more centuries, they are waiting for us to get smarter, and I swear to God, they will wait for a long time.

"Attention!"

"Fuck attention! What the fuck do you want now?!"

"Raise your head and stop bullshitting! Let's go!"

They set off. Some dragged themselves like beaten cats, shoving wrinkled dirty shirts into their pants and tightening their belts as they walked. Others were calm. And ready. They had some dull, fanatic looks, faces completely grown into a grimace that remained even when they slept. They were full of some supernatural strength, without a hint of fear, or their fear exclusively functioned as adrenaline.

There should be an equal opponent. One should have an equal oppo-nent. First, you compete in strength, craziness, and arguments. Then you drive him crazy, humiliate him, and in the end, you kill him. In the first ten seconds you feel indescribable grief. Afterwards, there is glory, pain, relief, and then emptiness.

They entered the village carefully, in pairs. It was quiet. Tins, rags, glass, dishes, pieces of furniture, a few corpses were scattered all around. Nothing unusual. There was a slight stench, but that was nothing compared to what it would be like when the Sun came out high and the temperature rose over 25 degrees.

The sky was an unreal blue, not a cloud in sight. Something moved underneath some half-charred jacket. With the tip of his rifle, he lifted the jacket lightly and met a green cat eye, wide open. There was neither the other eye nor an ear, a tail or both back legs. He was surprised that the cat made no sound at all, groan or meow. Nothing.

"You don't understand my rock 'n' roll, you damned animal…! I love you…"

Hasan-aga was stunned. As if God himself looked upon him through that free eye, and then…

He raised his head and saw that his partner had gone ahead a good distance, so he ran after him.

Soon they were with the rest of the group.

"Let's get out of here, there's nothing here."

"There's one crippled cat…"

"So, bring her home to your mother!"

He threw back the green glass bottle, and swallowed a few big mouthfuls.

"Uh! Good one!"

"Of course it's good, when there's nothing better! Though I wouldn't complain if some import dropped in, so we could treat ourselves!"

"Hey doc, got something for the head?"

"Doc has got it all bro, from shit to heroin, but it will cost you!"

"How much?"

"Well, I sort of like that crap you have around your neck, is that gold?"

"Aha, this is the only thing that's not for trade."

"Ah, everything is for sale, my friend, everything! When the ganja comes to its own, there is no sentimentality. Right now brother, if we weren't so tragic, we would be really comical. Me, in this trench, selling you this weed and with every passing second we could be blown to shit. Me and you… ha, ha… ah… ha, it would be the funniest if only I die and then you take everything, overdose, and then you're dead too… ha, ha, ha… ah, aha… ha, aha…

**

"I love you, you dumbass! I absolutely can't get it all out of my head! Neither those high waist panties of yours, turned gray from washing, nor that wide black T-shirt which you so quickly, almost shyly, throw on after sex, so I wouldn't see your excess weight under daylight... God, you stupid little girl, as if I didn't feel you with my entire being! I can't forget that gaze of yours as if it said: *Hey, I can't wait to come home and lay in bed, play Moore, and live it all over again!*

My baby, I want your fingers on my stomach again, do you remember, you said no one had a stomach like that... You wanted my hands to be like that, too. How many times you lectured me because of my cracked hands and bitten nails...

Realize, my dear, there's nothing in between, I know you want me, at least half as much as I want you, and we both know what a crazy time we live in, and that the Black devils are catching up to us, and that we can't run from them. They chase us like sheep, human stupidity is infinite, and we fight with all our might to stay normal, or at least not to cripple our memories. Come back! But I know you won't. You can't.

You've probably already folded me neatly into one of your drawers and started some new life far away, where people still think we live in tribes on the Balkans... but I don't judge them...

Come on, come back... let's live from today until tomorrow, because tomorrow won't come anyway. Let's look forward to every new morning, every shared cigarette, to comfortable, reminiscent darkness by the candles, and let's pretend the rest of the world doesn't exist. Because, my love, no one can steal our dreams.

I'm afraid of all these unfamiliar faces around me, all these 'new friends' and their cursed religions, and there's always more of them, always more..."

T. looked through the bars. A thin pigeon was walking on the edge of the window and he thought of how similar the two of them were. He returned to the couch and placed his hands on his knees. He was frightened, having felt the bone. He looked at his hands, then his leg, stood up, and began crying hysterically. His face was entirely twisted and hurting.

While he was playing as a kid in this very same basement, he would have never guessed that one day it would be his second home. Children laughed at old mister Nurko, who used to say: *"Get outta there kids, the basement isn't for playing, it's for, God forbid... play outside, there's the yard!"*

Mister Nurko was a skilled chess player; no one played chess better than he did. Some people bet big bucks on his victories. In the late 60s, he even shook Tito's hand when he came to visit the tall blast furnaces.

He and his wife, Mrs. Marija, had a big tapestry of Tile in their living room.

One day, while they were drinking their morning coffee, she told T.'s mother that she'd won first place in a competition for handmade work. She'd worked on that tapestry day and night. As soon as Mr. Nurko would leave for work, she would prepare lunch and grab that large piece of work.

Mrs. Marija and Mr. Nurko from the third floor had no children. While she was still young, Mrs. Marija had visited all of the doctors from Vardar to Triglav, i.e., from one part of the country to the other. She even went to church, lit a candle, and prayed to God to gift them a much-desired child. Even Mrs. Ševala, from the second floor, took her to a Khawaja who, as they said, was famous for solving those problems. In the end, she made peace with her fate, and the years made peace with theirs. That's why she loved us, the kids from the hall, as if we were her own, and no holiday would pass, religious or state, without her giving each child either a cookie or some other treat. She was even the main negotiator in T.'s house when T.'s old man would get wasted because he'd once again lost on a setup on the field and mistreated everyone around him.

Mrs. Marija didn't go down to the basement for a long time. She had a stroke, so she could barely get up to go to the toilet. Nurko was there regularly, like a conscientious and lifelong president of the homeowners' association, going down to the basement, making sure everything was functioning. Once, when those paramilitary men barged into people's houses, he saved Titoslav's old man from certainly being taken away, because he was dead drunk and talking nonsense again.

XIV

"Boredom is endless, and fear is even more infinite!" thought T. and didn't light a cigarette. And he wanted to smoke. Badly. He will have to stretch his legs and look for something to smoke. He couldn't go to his favorite café because it was closed (Sejo stirred up a quarrel with the thugs and loan sharks, so he had to hit the road). Hook-nose is dead and the caked-up blonde is banging with foreigners for cash. Still having three kilos of make up on her cheeks, hair dyed in an amateur way with washing soap and hydrogen, ten kilos lighter, and bags under her eyes, which a kilo of powder couldn't hide. And of course, drilled veins.

The underage waiter is rolling in cash. The other day he opened his own bar.

We will talk about the girls another time. His is somewhere across the pond anyway.

Studying. Judging by the way she was, I wouldn't be surprised to see her at CNN one day.

T. went down a narrow alley. Not a dealer in sight! He hasn't lit anything since the morning. There you have it, living in a town where weed is cheaper than a kilo of flour.

Ah, he is also crazy because he is mindlessly roaming the city like that.

"What's up, Hasan-aga?"

Tile got his nickname a long time ago, as a shear fuckery, while being on a "poetical" party where the girls gave each guy a nickname. And because T. had a hard-on for folk sayings of that time, he was named Hasan-aga.

"Hey Boki, how's it going, you got anything?"

"I've got nothing, Tile, and you're walking around like that, are you intentionally invoking the devil?"

"Can't sit at home anymore, listen to music or any other crap…"

"Did Mara hook you up with papers?"

"No, not yet, he said he will."

"And, your Bogdan, does he know anybody?"

"Ah, forget about my old man, he sees no further than the liquor. I'm surprised he is still alive. Shemsa has been tolerating him well all these years. They have become like two casualties. You don't know who is worse."

***

Dandy had been gone a long time. Did something happen to him?!

Maybe he's asleep, maybe dreaming… Actually, Dandy had been isolated for some time. To be honest, isolation didn't suit him at all. He made up things and thought more and more often about the story of THE TURNIP WITHOUT A ROOT. And he felt depressed. To clear some things up, here's that story:

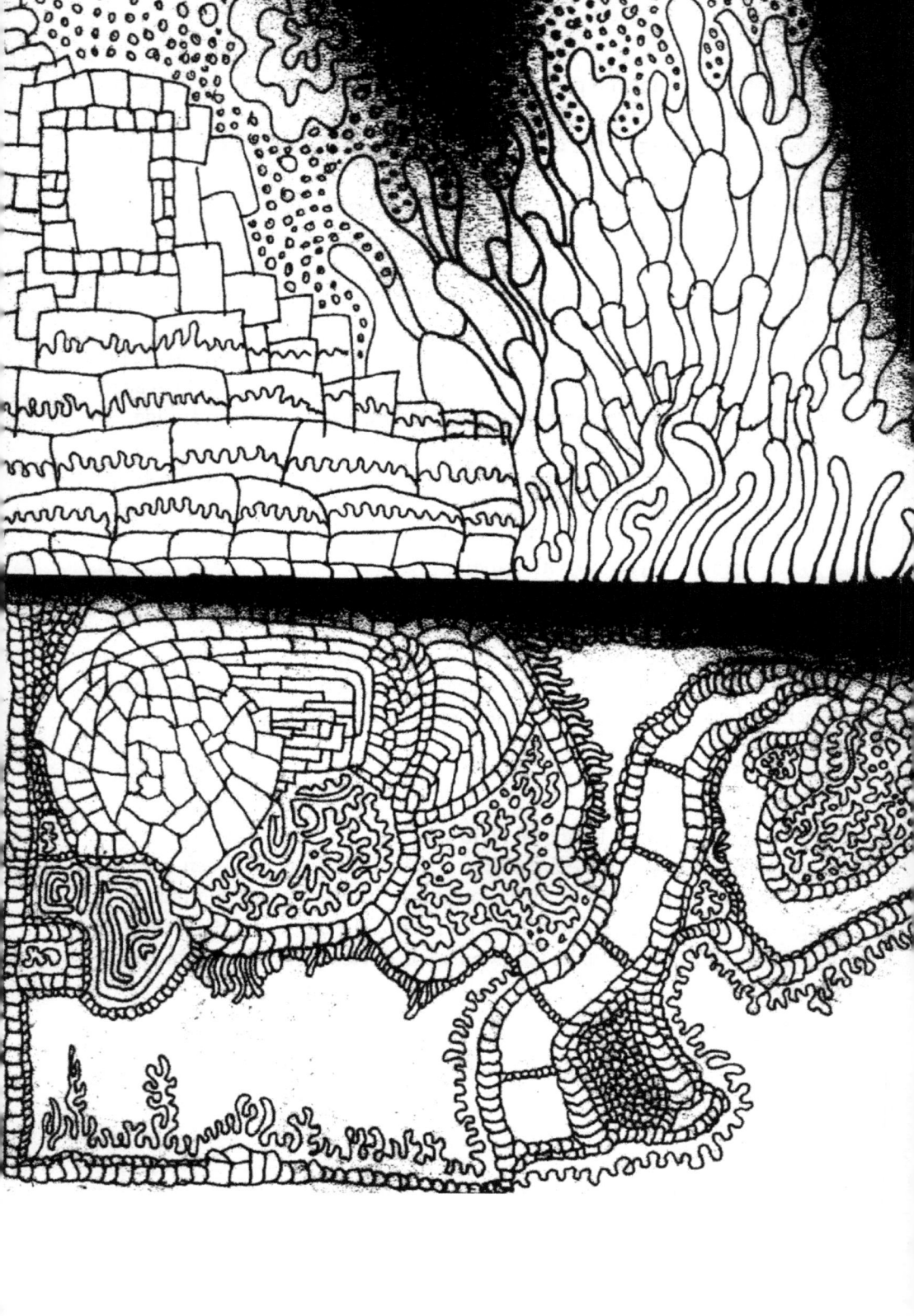

Turnip Without a Root

A big countryside landowner, whose flaws and virtues, oversights and merits will stay unbalanced until the end of this story, had a large turnip plantation. Each plant was similar to one another, they all grew at the same time, perhaps a bit dumb and uncreative, but let's call it free and happy. The landowner was watering them with exactly as much water as needed, so the periods of short-lived rain could do nothing to them. The turnips were growing; the landlord was taking care of them. He picked some and planted some, all that until one day.

Those days the drought was stronger than usual (which was incomprehensible for that well-behaved climate!). At the same time, the landowner was getting sick, his years were catching up to him as well as senility, anxiety, and weakness. All those changes were heavily reflected on his plantation. The landlord was no longer visiting his empire himself, instead he sent a servant who despised to water the plants one by one, so he would swing the bucket without taking care where the water would fall.

That's how the noticeable deviations happened on the plantation. Some turnips were big and great, full and heavy, some large in leaves, others tiny in the roots, and some had large, hollow roots and small, stunted leaves.

The first differences started to appear. The turnips that had already become pretty strong (either in leaves or roots), started to form the first turnip groups. The other turnips, hoping for rain, quickly pulled into them. Big and great turnips soon made alliances with the landlord's servant (that's what they called it, although it's known to everyone that plants can't speak with people or make alliances with them).

As time passed, the turnip groups grew larger, the landlord was older and sicker, and in the end he died. The servant then abandoned the plantation completely, so its condition became even stranger. The large turnips distributed water as they pleased, and they were actually quite pissed. In fact, the entire plantation turned into a bunch of deformed and sad turnips which persistently and, in every way, tried to get around in that jungle (we're calling the plantation a jungle because besides the turnips it was inhabited by all kinds of weeds, which had used this stress to grow to unseen proportions).

A small number of younger turnips remained stunned, lost. Until recently, they had planned an uprising against dumb and uncreative growth and now it turned out they were complaining for their old order. Absolutely ridiculous! There were those among them who rose their leaves high to the clouds, hoping not for rain but a flood. Their roots were small and stunted, but they held them roughly to the ground, not even giving them a single tendon.

As it normally happens in these stories, there is always one amongst a hundred, and so it is in this story as well. That one specimen is not alone, there were many similar ones, but they were scattered all around the plantation. There was no way for them to organize and pull off something useful, because in the general chaos that appeared any attempt at positive organization was doomed to fail.

So, as I've said, among those turnips there was one that would remain without a root. In the beginning, our turnip hero had belonged to the group that was in favor of collapsing the old order, so he felt lost and abandoned in these new changes. Suddenly, he found himself (like most, although he didn't want to admit it) without anything, not just without water and life space, but without anything he'd once believed, whether it was insane and wrong or not.

He tried desperately to join some of the newly formed turnip groups, but it didn't work. Some of them had excessively pumped roots, although inside they was gelatinous and fake. Others had enormous leaves, wide and strong. They resisted wind and drought attacks as if it was a normal thing. Their roots were small, but they were of great importance to them.

Our turnip hero didn't like either of the two, or the fifth, or the tenth. And they, in return, found one hundred and one flaws in him. At first, he persistently tried to find similarities between his and their roots and leaves, comparing the color, size, weight, fullness, and who knows what. But something was always missing. If only he could take little bits out of everyone! Then he would surely be able to make a group in which he would fit in. But to no success. Then our hero tried to live a lonely life, but it was even worse.

Days were passing and the turnip hero became more and more sad. One day, a ruckus was heard from the landlord's house (in which the servant was well accommodated). And at last! The turnip hero heard a familiar and, in that moment, very dear voice. It was the voice of Arnold Schwarzenegger in the Conan or Terminator movies.

Our hero livened up, spinning a few times around his axis, the roots snapped (surrounding turnip groups grabbed and tousled him), and the hero ran in the direction of the music and cried in turnip tongue:

"*Yeeeeaaaaaaaaahhhhh!!!*"

***

Fieewwwwwwwwwwww!

"Hey, all these stars are blasting through at 300 km/h. It doesn't matter. I don't know how to drive a car by these rules. But then again, if I'm driving my car on the left side, I don't know if that is right? Better to drive on the right side. And what if an accident happens?! Nothing! Get out of the car and pick up the person involved in the accident. Then take him to the first four-leaf clover. He's good, you're good. Afterwards play dumb and search for a three-leaf clover."

"Ah, yes!"

"Ay, ay, Corto Maltese, did you have to show up in this comic?! Can't you see there aren't any pictures in it, just a lot of stupid exclamation marks! Without screams!"

Dandy laughed, spat out a booger from the bottom of his lungs, and thought that there wasn't even a trace of femininity in him! Right afterwards, he pulled a white piece of chalk out of his pocket. He drew a hopscotch, then instead of numbers he only drew nines. And just like that, he started jumping in his socks and mumbling the nursery rhyme:

Nothing with anything x 9

Head in the bag x 9

Final word x 9

And full stop x 9

Bad legs x 9

Steady pace x 9

072 x 9

No regrets x 9

With a line x 9

Slow game x 9

Quick rhythm x 9

Conformity x 9… I want to slide…

Bing! Bang! Bang! And Dandy ended up in a dumpster with withered flowers on his head and a piece of apple between his teeth. He got up, dusted himself off, laughed happily like a child, and left.

Our turnip hero felt, pretty much in THE BIG WORLD, the same as Dandy was feeling in this game. Which means, completely confused and awkward, but quite free and hopeful.

XV

T. has been shaking from the cold for hours. There, the moments of his weakness had come. He was scared. Scared! Purely for the purpose of forgetting, he began piecing together some "philosophic" thoughts. As if he were some big thinker in a transitioning time of human history, talking nonsense.

In a moment of weakness,
when the head mixes with the conflict (and fear mixes with an ordinary moment),
the bad needs space.
Because mixing is an answer but not the solution.
The solution is in the hands
and in the laundry which swings on the drying rack on minus infinity.
"Hey, this isn't too bad!"

In a moment of weakness, when the head mixes with the Conflict, and FEAR with an ordinary moment and Habit, the Devil needs space, because conserving a healthy mind is an answer but NOT the solution. The solution is in YOUR hands. Which means, take your dirty laundry, and wash it YOURSELF, and choose a positive direction for sailing. If there isn't one, create it…

When Dandy went into isolation, someone who wanted to imitate him appeared in T.'s surroundings. This, let's call him Pseudo Dandy, was actually the Devil's envoy, which means one sad and unfortunate Homo sapiens specimen. He openly cooperated with Fear and Paranoia. His pressure on T. normally consisted of threats without basis or reason, and degradation of basic human rights (which are, of course, a relative thing!).

His words were like:

"T., you are half man, half brute! People like you are an embarrassment for Our Civilization!

How was it even allowed for such mutants to be born? You and others like you should be locked in a ghetto and burnt once and for all!"

T. felt repulsion toward that idiot, he felt sorry for him, and he was afraid of him. In the beginning, he tried to enter the psychology of that Pseudo Dandy, he banged his head, contemplated, got angry, was afraid, he hated and he cried, but in the end he shrugged his shoulders and said to himself:

THE WORLD IS FULL OF UNFORTUNATE PEOPLE.

THERE ARE NO GOOD AND BAD ONES.

THERE ARE ONLY LUCKY AND UNLUCKY ONES.

Little Story No. 2

How foolishly you laughed! You were usually speaking quickly, incoherently, jumping from topic to topic. Basically, it all came down to hollow feministic theories, which, as you said yourself, don't exist. Actually, the more you doubted them, the harder you tried to convince your interlocutor otherwise. Ah, you were afraid! You were afraid of your femininity, which tirelessly poked out from underneath your every cuss, your desperate walk, grimaced face, and slouched shoulders.

Ha, ha, ha, you were eating like a mason, shoving massive piles of meat pie in your mouth, and you could never run! And you always had to pee! Whenever we entered somewhere for the first time, you would first inform yourself where the toilet was. Ah, the toilet was your empire! Your oasis of intimacy, a petrol station for your soul and body. A place to take a breath in exchange for an oxygen tank. You would sometimes stay there for hours, sitting half naked on the toilet bowl or brushing your teeth for an eternity, mumbling to yourself obscenities in the mirror. And then, the showering! You would let a far stream of nearly steaming water run across your back, draining the heater to the last drop (members of your family were regularly pissed in front of your locked bathroom door!).

You despised all forms of makeup and jewelry. In your opinion, those were self-conscious and unskilled attempts of imperfect women to complete themselves. You were never interested in fashion either. Sometimes I thought that you were actually envious of those attractive dolls in town, although you never (not at all!) wanted to be like them. Even when all those players from your dreams picked up those same dolls, you exclaimed with repulsion that all men were dumb cattle who couldn't stand a woman with character! Ha ha ha! And you added that all of that dumb cattle thought exclusively with their dicks!

As much as you tried to hide it, a more experienced player like myself could tell you weren't a bad pussy.

You romantic idiot. I just wanted to fuck you! Nothing more. What had you thought up in your head? I could never love a woman like you!

***

"Get up, you drunken animal! If we miss again, it's over!"

Hasan-aga twitched and realized he'd been thinking about the past more and more often. He was convinced the cause was that mini-break. How could a couple of days spent in a different environment totally throw a man off balance?!

It was easier for him here. There was no place for hesitation in the black and white world. Either you're alive or you're not. There is no third way. And there is no tomorrow. Or today. Everything is now. And it will be so for who knows how long, and that's not even important anymore. Because Hasan-aga is a man from the black and white world of eternal battle (regardless of whether it makes sense or not) and he could not make his way in this colorful world, full of tiny deceits. He was hard and rude to those in the colorful world, and they were uncomfortable because of his behavior, for he usually said what they kept to themselves.

He took women roughly, like an animal, as if he was punishing them for their romance. But then, the easy ones he loved gently, resting on their prematurely aged breasts. Actually, in those few timeless days he'd managed to hurt all those who loved him before his departure. He despised all those people who reminded him of the past, all those who lived by the calendar, thus creating some irritating discomfort.

***

"Who is normal? Is anyone even normal?!"

There are no normal ones. Everyone is ordinary. At times, T. would become very cynical. It was stronger than him. Actually, he'd programmed himself, he no longer counted hours and, if possible, he was on the move the whole day. He invented new hobbies, for example, playing chess with Mr. Nurko or eternally solving mathematical problems. All these eternal calculations gave him a much-needed sense of control.

He didn't communicate with his housemates. Actually, for the first time, they accepted each other as they were and no one maltreated anyone. Only on the morning when Mirna (Titoslav's younger sister) said that Mladen (her boyfriend) had finally solved the scheme for them to set off to Croatia and somehow get their hands on Italy, he felt some unfamiliar sadness, although relief as well. Mirna was his only ally in the house. And the smartest. She was one of the youngest children (and there weren't many of them) whom they didn't manage to spoil. The old man never looked sideways at her, let alone snap or beat her. Actually, she was one of those girls everyone loved. With some invisible magic, she managed to get under everyone's skin. No one ever hurt her, no one, of course, except that hillbilly of hers! "Her Mlađo," a petty criminal and a coarse guy, was taking Mirna for everything, leaving her nothing.

While she was extremely smart, she was extremely stupid concerning men. And maybe Mlađo was some good fuck, so much so that Mirna came the first time they had banged. And we all know how first impressions are important to chicks. So she forgave him for his lack of general education, trips with the local vultures, and his insane family.

He did everything someone loaded with money would do. His family was always wealthy. Mlađo spun a family business which consisted of stealing money from the people: buying everything in town for as cheap as possible (and we know that everything is for sale during a war) and reselling the same items outside of town for big bucks. Although, to some people that was the only way to get food or to leave. Women loved him like crazy, whether for his money or for his beauty.

So, that morning, Mirna had informed the household that she would be leaving in the afternoon. And she left. She arrived in Italy only three years later, when she'd finally had enough. Mlađo had stayed in Zagreb, started his own firm, and began beating her. Toni, who was almost two years old when he left with his mother, now calls Mirna's second husband (a mild, fifteen years older Slovenian) dad. Mom was crying the entire day, and dad and her brother were pretending that nothing had happened.

The day when Zvjezdan (Tile's two years older brother) showed up at home, carrying two kilograms of Danish feta, salty as poison, four tins without labels, a kilogram of rice, and a kilogram of macaroni, Tile knew that Jezdi had got a job from the foreigners. There he will finally cash in on all those hours spent on translating Dylan's songs, while his pals were getting drunk in the park.

He died in a rather foolish way, catching a stray bullet from a town gang confrontation.

T.'s relations with his brother were tepid. Jezda had normally played the elder, smarter brother, who held lectures about morality, reporting to dad each of Tisi's action. In fact, he loved and directed his younger brother in the most difficult way. They had absolutely nothing in common, apart from a similar taste in music.

In those times, T. had lived entirely without plans. He didn't want to change, not now, when everything was changing. In those self-pity moments, he wished to die quickly of natural causes. He sped up the aging process, but in vain. Only his eyes looked older and more tired.

"God, will this shit ever stop! I'm sick of this anxiety!" Dandy said. He folded the wings into his bag and left. T. took a deep breath, pulled a sheet over his back, and fell into a deep, dreamless sleep.

XVI

"Do you know I am really annoyed by your stupid babbling?! How can you talk so much?! You and your democratic decisions! Can't you see I'm stressed?! I don't know where my head is, and I'm crazy. And you're not far either…"

He loved Little Girl infinitely. Just enough so he could bite her soul once and for all during one occasion when he came home for a short time. And he didn't even notice it, which was worst of all.

They were something like soulmates, exchanging positive energy, pals.

"Tile, stop bullshitting, drink that beer so we can leave! I can't look at these caked up faces! Where did you find this café?! Couldn't you have found a more pompous place? Look, look at that slicked guy! And look at his buddy, ha, ha, ha, all would-be alternatives!!"

"Little Girl, fuck them all, look at the chicks over here! I don't know which one's better… ugh!"

***

Dandy, quaking with fear, exchanged a game with Bad.

It looked like a man on a chair in a large room with a high ceiling where the light was shining only on it. The man was one of those people whose age couldn't be determined, neither by his hair, nor by his face. His body was hidden in the suit by which you couldn't tell his status, profession, or age.

Now we should write about Dandy's aches which were taking some special shapes lately. They were no longer strokes. Every day they would turn into a tiring game of endurance and fortitude. And because Dandy was one dangerous hypochondriac, he was convinced that he had some incurable disease.

Dandy once started a conversation like this with Bad:

"Come on, Bad, don't make me beg you!"

"Dandy, don't take this so personally, don't you understand this is a collective hysteria I am participating in and that you and everyone else are just a job I have to do. I'm here to hurt. That's my only job…"

Game

Imagine one room full of school things, outfits worn only once, thrown over a chair, walls full of newspaper cutouts, surprising drawings and some shocking songs, controversial mottos, old worn-out toys, and gurgling of water in the radiators.

Well, one gramophone lives in such a room. It's an old, khaki colored machine which lives from games.

Games of records of all ages and preservation, old singles and new LP's, scratched and without shine, singles without cases. The gramophone was much more durable than a CD player. Much more selective, more just. Its sound had something special, something that CD's will never have. It was something persistent, something so emotional and provincial, a little bit raw, but honest.

"*... allow me to introduce myself, I hope you're guessing my name, but what surprises you is the nature of my game...*" sang the good old LP, playing circles, perfection, infinity, eternity. It toyed with laughter, crying, mortal pathetic, jealousy, love, pride, and some entirely ordinary happiness.

All in all, it was like one good bang that was a game, like any important thing in life. Everything good is a fair play and in a circle. A game of turning, being born, dying, growing and being moody, dancing, a game of good and evil. The only difference was in the time and speed of the game and the turning.

It's like when you put the LP to 45 spins. That creates distortion, abortion, depression, lies, fall of objectivity, pain, deception, a sad clown with a big blue tear drawn under his eye. Or a funeral in a big communal tomb for the poor during insane rain which doesn't stop. A power outage creates silence, tragedy, sadness. Clean and sterile.

"Darling, beware of transience and oblivion... you don't know how much they hurt..."

With those random sentences Dandy finished his story to a little bird, a story about a game, so similar to all the stories in this world.

***

"Listen T., I really can't do this anymore. Talk to me! Hey, it's me!"

Hasan-aga looked at Little Girl with some crazy eyes, unaware he'd scared her with that look.

"How come you don't recognize me?!"

"Hey, I'm leaving, and you see what you're going to do…"

***

Dandy was still nervous. His stomach hurt, the only organ he had.

"The world is empty! The world is THE DAY AFTER. Only cockroaches and the sand will survive."

XVII

He'd been awake for almost ten minutes, but he didn't dare to open his eyes.

"God, what if I can't see!"

The pictures of the last few days passed through his head like thunder… action… suddenly a bang… and then darkness… Nothing… There is nothing there!

"Only darkness and indifference. There, that is salvation."

He thinks, so he is alive. Slowly, with the tips of his fingers, he touched the cold iron edge of the bed. Chills went through him. He felt no pain. Suddenly a sharp smell of chemicals roughly itched his nose. So, his nose, fingers, and brain work. Now the eyes. Should he open both of them at once or slowly, one by one? Ah, he'll do it all at once, whatever happens…

Darkness, darkness!!! He hadn't even managed to fully panic and was already slowly discerning things through the mist: first the wall connecting to the ceiling, then the top of the window to the right, the treetop in a hospital park a little lower, then a long filthy terrace even lower. A deep, tobacco-burnt voice coming from his left jerked him from his sightseeing:

"Ah you can sleep a lot, it's a miracle! Swear to God, they got you well.

We'd had a lot of fuck about you. I barely patched you up. Luckily, we had blood, otherwise… Come on, say something, your tongue is intact, does it hurt?"

Hasan-aga tried to smile, but that smile contorted into a painful expression. Not ordinary pain, but the other kind. He looked up and saw Dandy, who said:

46

MIMA MIHAJLOVIĆ,

"The more it hurts you, the less it hurts me. Everything in this world is constant. If you're sleeping here now, that means that someone in, let's say, Bolivia is awake, or if you're crying, then someone in Africa is laughing, or if you're here receiving a liter of blood, then someone somewhere in Asia probably lost it, and maybe even died. Don't worry, it's all just a game, a game of endurance and fortitude, and when a man thinks he can take no more, then it all twists like a rag and there's always a few more drops of water. It's all, my dear friend, a game, game, game..."

Dandy laughed loudly (in that same moment some child in Azerbaijan got slapped by their mother and cried bitterly) and began his lullaby:

Nothing with anything x 9
Everything with infinity x 9
Head in the bag x 9
Hands in the water x 9...

***

"How long have I been here?!"
"This is the eleventh day."
"Who are you?"
"A GHOST."
"Aha. Are you going to take me away now?"
"No. I'm just playing with you. You're not mine, I don't want you."
"Why? Am I worth so little?!"
"No. You carry with you something I don't like."
"What?"
"Irony."

***

They told him nothing and he didn't ask anything. Neither how he was doing nor when he was going to get up, or if he would even get up. He was adjusting slowly. But it didn't last for a long time. Someone told him she was there... He didn't see her for two years. Too familiar words were buzzing in his head, but now, the whole eternity was separating them.

"I'm going. And you know that. Because the time has come to go our own ways..."

And hers:

"I know and I say I hate it! Because I can't do anything about it, and I'm scared…"

No, he wasn't dreaming. It was all too real. His will was stronger, he got up.

XVIII

They lay next to each other. Calm. He gently stroked her hair and said:

"Shh, don't, everything is okay…"

Tears were running down her cheeks and she repeated:

"I can't believe it… I can't… believe it…"

He'd changed. Forever. But he still loved Little Girl.

"You don't need to tell me anything, if you don't want to…"

"I don't."

"Do you hate me?"

"No, you silly girl."

"I thought you would be rude again and talk a lot, like before. No, I thought there was no hope. I thought you had gone. And it's all so weird, yet so right… I love you…"

He didn't say anything. He only pulled her closer to himself as if they would lose each other again and he didn't want to think about anything.

Blood is one. There is one blood. And it's the same for all of us.

That was all he thought before desire arose in him again…

The Day Before

I feel you. I feel your smell all around me. I feel it on my hands, I know you're here, you're close. I am no longer the same. Believe me, there are no days on which I don't wonder how it would have been like if we had stayed close forever, but we were children then and everything was different. The future looked pink, we were free, young, and had something in front of us. You know the real truth, but it was too cruel, and I didn't want to accept it. I believed no one could steal our dreams.

By defending myself from you, I thought I was defending myself from the Truth. But unsuccessfully. You can't run away from Fear. It always catches up to you.

I am different now. Better said, the remainder of a former spirit in fine armor, which is slowly withering while time is treading on us. And the waiting. Time flies without a hint of a guilty conscience. And it hurts. A lot.

Throughout all the cities I've passed, and all the people I've met, I always left behind a part of myself. And now I am empty. And calm. I packed everything in the brain's cubbyholes, put everything in drawers. And therefore, don't say anything, forget prejudices. We are just two emotional cripples and we rely on each other during this small break, which has no time and space. Don't say anything, just love me the whole night…

The Day After

I'm coming back. You know I can't stay. This isn't my soil, I can't get around here.

I know that you aren't a good memory or a pathetic consolation to a soldier. But that's how it is. I can't change anything there. You are not Hasan-aga's wife with a bunch of smudged kids, whose years match the husband's absence.

Get out of here! Go! Moments are important. They're the only thing that matters in life. They hold us in life. Them and hope. Leave this hell and save, at least, a bit of what you have. My dear, there is but one life and don't ever forget that, not even when you're sad again one day… or happy…

***

"Wake up! Hey, wake up, we're here!"

And again… from the beginning. Blood, earth, and life. All from the start again… I am again in my own hell.

"I love you, you fool…"

Dandy held out well. He walked, he sang again, and wrote letters.

He remembered. No, that wasn't healthy, but still…

***

Nothing is more beautiful than a million drops and all blue. Nothing is more beautiful than that first thing you see when you dive out from the blue infinity. And the Sun. And the salt on your face that burns because of the heat. And the sky. And freedom. Broadness, space, blue, blue…

YOU ARE FREE WHEN YOU HAVE NOTHING TO LOSE!

***

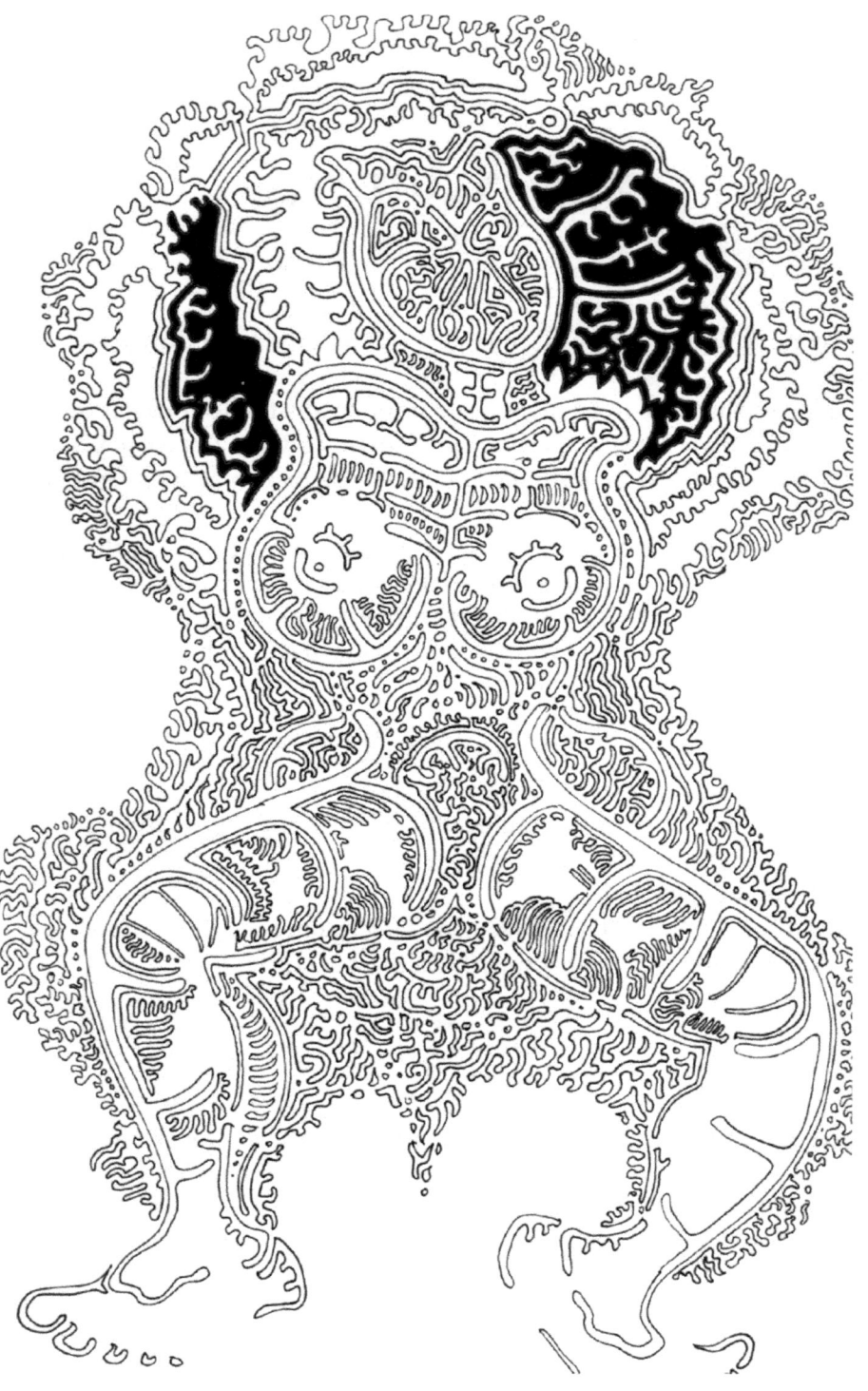

We've left out Fear in this story a bit, but not because it got lost, but because it's in that crystal phase now. It sleeps. Like a virus. So be quiet, quiet so as not to wake it. Shhh!

XX

Tisi had, by some delightful miracle, survived this Balkan war. He'd returned home on a rather ordinary day, long after the Dayton Agreement. In his house he found only his old man (what irony, the old tragic drunk had made it, that crumb of a liver was miraculously still working). His old lady died quietly, as she was living, although cancer had ruined her body, and sadness for her children tore at her soul. She'd never complained about any pain, although, already sick at the time of Zvjezdan's funeral, they'd barely pulled her away from his freshly dug grave.

Aunt Azra had nourished her until her last day, running from one end of the town to the other, chasing medicine over some connections at the hospital full of wounded people (morphine nowhere to be found!).

One morning, she'd just told the aunt that she didn't want a religious funeral, because if there were a God, he wouldn't allow someone to suffer like this. The old man wasn't home, when he returned after, mom was no longer there. Mirna had made it just in time for the funeral, travelling with a small child over hills and mountains with some new corridors leading to her hometown, and Tisi wasn't even there. They informed him ten days later, because no one could find him.

The old man had, having been left alone, drank all the money Mirna had sent (secretly from her frantic husband) in seven days, and he never had a hard time asking for more.

There you fucking go, some people never learn to take care of themselves and some children forever remain parents to their parents. And so, Mirna had taken care of her old man until his death, bearing through all his whims, probably, to some extent, due to a guilty conscience.

Having come "home," Titoslav looked carefully through the walls, closets and doors, looking for something, probably looking for himself, or at least some memories of his old self. Everything once familiar (it was all in the same condition because aunt Azra had, even after the death of her sister, continued to visit Bogdan, to clean his apartment or to cook something from time to time, thus risking another fight with her husband) now seemed somehow foreign and strange, as if he hadn't grown up there, but someone with his name and surname did.

He slept pretty poorly, either because of the silence or his leg which had never healed properly.

He and his old man were barely talking. And they never had anything to say to each other. Both led their own lives.

Time was passing, and Tisi was slowly getting used to the silence around him. He rarely went out.

He usually spent his time sitting in his room, smoking, reading some old, nebulous books and fighting with his nightmares. Actually, he made a kind of a quarantine, being aware that the adjustment phase wouldn't pass so easily or quickly. Luckily, he didn't go for narcotics (God knows why!), he was high even without them! As if he was slowly waking from some strange dream, known only to him. And he was smart enough not to have much contact with people.

Dandy still hadn't contacted him from his asylum or quarantine, so it was okay.

Mirna called him regularly to come over, sent warranty letters a few times, begging and promising, but he felt as though something was telling him it was not time yet.

One morning, when his self-pity had reached its peak, he went outside and was standing on the bridge for a long time, thinking about jumping down. Just at that moment, Dandy appeared:

"What is it, pussy, did you shit yourself, huh? You don't have the balls to kill yourself. Ah, my old pal, you need courage for that. You would love to jump most of all and to have some crazy fate to save you again, so that some commotion could be raised around you again!"

"Dandy, quit bullshitting! I'm sick of all of it… Look at me…"

"As if you're the only one! Look around you, you egoistic fool! Everything's gone to shit! You think all these people around you have it easy?! Look at them, look! They're just shadows of their former personalities and stories. But they are not pussies like you! They have hope! Miserable, worthless, crippled, and suspicious, but they have it! They've found a straw to hold onto, so they're dangling. They know very well that it won't get better in the next twenty years, but they're holding in."

"Go away, you insane fucking bastard, I hate you, I hate all of you, and I hate Mirna with her stupid stories! As if I can just leave this fucking country cold-bloodedly, go fucking abroad, and pretend like nothing happened! I CAN'T!"

"Well, of course you can't when you're afraid! You need to start over again and a wussy like you doesn't dare, you're afraid to leave your self-pity, you masochist. There will be no one to feel sorry for you, so jump then, what are you waiting for?!!!"

"I'm waiting for the rain to fall…"

XXI

The alarm clock was ringing persistently, and its irritating sound pierced everything in the room. The girl snoozed it who knows how many times, desperately stealing another minute.

"It's the same every morning! Is there a worse moment of the day than this?! Does the Sun ever shine in this country?! I'm so sleepy… ah…"

The girl stood up and walked tentatively to the bathroom. She sat on the toilet and almost fell asleep again. She looked at the clock in the hallway and was stunned:

"Ugh, fuck, 7.15 a.m. already! I will never learn to get up on time," she thought.

"Ah no daylight in sight, utter darkness! I want to get enough sleep at least once!"

She was slowly but surely getting used to certain constants, just regularly monkeying around a little bit (until she gets screwed once). Life in the distant Wonderland was like a home to her, probably the only real one, after all those adventures in foreign comics and movies, where God himself was probably watching over her. And now she was great, calm, complaining about the darkness and rain, but she regularly got up for work every morning. And she gets drunk on the weekend, like the rest of the normal world.

There's not much to be told here. We all know very well the stories of provincial girls that grew up too soon in the big, wide world.

T. and the girl haven't seen each other for years. Except for that entirely ordinary afternoon, when the girl decided to leave (actually, the decision had quite accidentally fallen on Wonderland) – on that same afternoon when her impatient soles started to itch her. Tisi was still in a black and white jungle. Nevertheless, they thought about each other. For at least three minutes a day.

She would sometimes have a pubescent fantasy, imagining herself and Tisi in an entirely different time and space (as it normally is in fantasies).

In those fantasies of hers they were always on the top floor of some building, in a room which unbelievably reminded her of some smell from her childhood.

It's likely that our entire emotional life is one big sensory fantasy, where we watch everything from an extremely subjective angle.

She regularly made friends with people like herself, smelling them like a tracking dog. How good it was to find people with the same mindset, blind fans and super-egos (neglecting the ego). It was like rebirth!

And there were many of them, of all races and nations, genders, age, and class. She sorted them all neatly into drawers and romantically kept contact with them, even after many years.

And she'd sorted Tisi into one of those unaware mindset ones with a special stamp of devotion. And he hated people like that! He was never, nor would he ever be, a part of that world! To him, they were unreliable and full of themselves, he judged them with all possible human laws. Regarding that question, Tisi was a real Westerner.

Actually, Little Girl was feverishly attracted to those clever, raw Westerners, just like every feminist pussy who was turned on by a brute!

***

Tisi didn't jump from the bridge, and Little Girl didn't come to her hometown for six years.

Finally, after the crazy journeys all around, the road finally led her more south (she was completely driven insane by some crazy adrenaline, some wild nostalgia, completely blind to reality), where a meeting with Tisi, after a dangerous dose of alcohol and some cheerful, homegrown ganja, finished almost tragically.

She had never known how to stop trying her luck. She adored that balancing on the edge and forgetting about everything. She enjoyed every moment in a suicidal way and, to his big surprise, she'd knocked Tisi out of his shoes entirely. Hey, he thought he was clinically dead!

In the end, he didn't know anymore whether to love her or to beat her, both would've given him the same satisfaction. She'd brazenly become involved in his life again (neither was he innocent, he let her in slowly, through the back entrance!). She'd shaken all his middle paths, and she shook her own, too! That tiny dose of masochism excited and scared her at the same time, and it gave a new dimension to everything.

No, they didn't bang, only God knows why! Ah, probably only because of technical reasons…

And this story would probably have some other ending then.

Because you can bang a good friend only once. Each other time it would be pure maltreatment.

My dear, imagine a circle and us spinning and spinning fast. Imagine, everything around us losing its shape, everything becoming a colorful pantomime and there is a humming in our ears. And nothing can be seen, except your smiling eyes, and nothing can be heard, except your smile. We're holding hands, firmly, our fingers going numb, our knees getting weak, we're losing balance, but we don't stop. I'm yelling, loudly, but I can't hear my voice, only you can hear the cry, and you're laughing, laughing, without end…

***

T. turned around. He cheated God. He looked for a particular answer and direction, but he didn't look at the signs, instead he sunk like a cork tied to a stone and thrown in the water. The cork tried to stay on the surface, but the stone kept pulling it down. He says he had no choice. Maybe he didn't, who knows!

T.'s story is a sad one and similar to all the other stories in this world. And I don't know how it ends. Because of some technical reasons.

***

Torn between two worlds, both his but both foreign, Dandy was crying and laughing at the same time. But then, he was poised like the handwriting of his language, which was now someone else's.

Torn between two eternal loves, he searched for the stronger, measuring on a scale which one was more truthful.

He searched for the hills in a straight field, but there were none there, of course. And there in the hills, he smelled everything and waited for everything to become straight. But it didn't.

Torn between himself and himself, he waited. As so many times until then. He waited for the sun, he was completely awake and aware. And he waited and waited and waited, waited… Waited for T. to come HOME…

He thought that the house, conformism of the close type, could maybe be moved to some specified (or unspecified!) time. Maybe T. had moved his house into some other life, maybe a life out of a movie or a comic.

***

Because we've lost our main hero in the mass of entirely ordinary stories, it's time to move onto other similar stories. Just for variety's sake.

Little Deny, Titoslav's neighbor from the other entrance of the same building, was a youngster when the shit started. He'd just turned twelve, lit his first cigarette, and drank two bottles of beer with the local rascals in front of the building. His folks were very nice people, ambitious. His old man was made fun of for being henpecked because he was regularly seen throwing out the trash, stringing up the laundry on the balcony, overly washing his car, dragging bags from the market and the shop, and driving around his mother-in-law and wife to their business. His mother-in-law, Rabija, regularly snuck rags from Turkey, dressing the whole neighborhood. She was usually sitting at hairdresser Nevenka's salon the whole day, drinking the fiftieth cup of coffee, taking out her bags and little bags and showing them to her.

"Mira, my dear, look at these pants, they're the latest fashion. I have two more."

"Wait, let me call my Sandra so she can try them on right away!" she dials the number with Nevenka's phone and yells into the speaker: "Sandra, child, it's me. Did you have breakfast? Aha, aha… I'm at Nena's in her salon… Come down, Mrs. Rabija brought lots of things that you can try on if you want… What?! Put him on the phone right away… Sasha, what did I say?! No playing ball in the house!!!"

Neighbor Jasmina, Deny's mother, was one of those energetic women who always got what they wanted. She and Zoka (the father) had been together just five months before their wedding (because Jasmina's stomach had already become visible), but evil tongues say that she got pregnant to spite her mother and father because Zoka wasn't a suitable son-in-law, even though he was an engineer. And who knows what his folks would say about Jasmina if they were alive. When Deny was born, everything was smoothed out. Rabija got her long-awaited grandson, so she and Zoka got along in the end, and grandfather Ibro cooled off as well.

Deny was overly pampered, he was always sickly because he had chronic bronchitis. Every winter the doctor prescribed going to the sea, so Deny went to the Adriatic coast with his mother and grandfather a few times a year. And when he was a bit older, Jasmina still brought him dry undershirts whenever they went to someone's house as guests. The plans for Deny's future as an only child and the only grandson were, of course, unlimited and unrealistic. Deny was dangerously annoyed by that even as a kid. All of the other children were playing in front of the building, while he had to go to guitar classes (although, when he grew up a bit, that guitar got him his

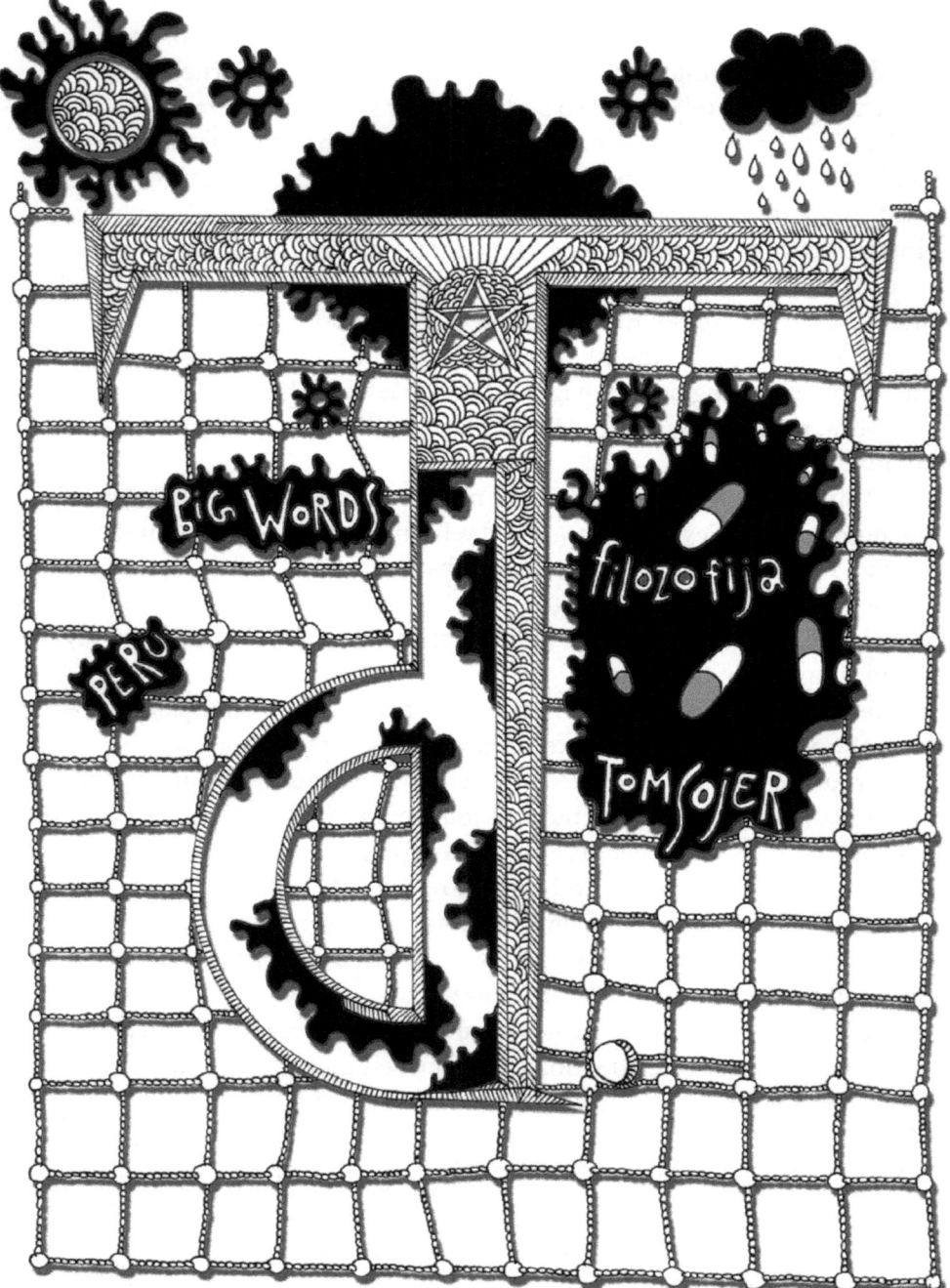

first girl). All the children sliding down the slope behind their building in plastic milk crates wearing ripped and used up gloves, while he went skiing in Slovenia.

And then his garbs, which his father brought back from his official trips, were from abroad. In short, Deny lived like a little aristocrat in a workers' settlement because his mother didn't want to move to the capital city, although his father had offers to move there for a better paid job. Jasmina had to go to her mother's for a cup of coffee every day. She ran to Rabija every day after work, carrying shopping bags, and then dragging home her mother's sarma (sauerkraut leaves stuffed with minced meat) and baklava. And of course, inevitable Sunday lunch at her parent's. That could be missed only if, God forbid, someone was deadly sick. And every time it was the same ritual, soup with homemade noodles, pie, roasted meat and potatoes, cakes, coffee, mild teasing of their son-in-law, but all within cultural boundaries (because they had to sit at that same table again next week). Then, arguing between mother and daughter – about whether Deny had to eat a full plate or whether he could leave something for later, and the wise silence of old Ibro and his occasional lifting of the head from the daily newspaper, to give them both piercing gazes.

And because of Jasmina's excessive commitment to her parents, even though a job in Germany was already waiting for Zoka, they had almost stayed in Bosnia when the shit started. When they moved to the country of Disneyland and chubby people after three years, she didn't calm down until she brought her parents over the pond. Poor people almost died from the sadness in a foreign world. They neither spoke to anyone in that damned foreign language nor did they drink coffee. And when old Ibro had a heart attack and barely made it, he finally lost it, so he told Jasmina and Zoran that he wouldn't die in another's world, picked up his old lady and went home. Jasmina began crying and begging, stating the advantages of the Western world, good doctors and full shops, but the old man stuck to his decision.

The daughter finally made peace with her parent's decision, packed them a full shitload of western things, a microwave, a coffee machine, magic pots that cooked by themselves, electric toothbrushes and electric blankets, devices for massaging the back and feet... and a computer with a web camera so they could see each other daily. Even Zoka had given them a short course about using the PC, to which, after a long deprecation and fear of the unknown, they finally agreed, even though they didn't understand a thing.

Deny became a pretty boy, a little spoiled and a little romantic, good in school and good at basketball. The mother worked in a hospital, forever sore that they hadn't accepted her dentist diploma. Instead, she was washing the butts of sick German grandmothers. And nothing happened regarding Zoka's promised job, except for toiling on a construction site from dusk till dawn.

Deny behaved as if none of that was his business, he went to school and his trainings and only sometimes some sadness would awaken in him, usually when he ran into a misunderstanding of his romantic nature.

He thought he would stay there forever, so he greeted the trip to the "promise land" completely unprepared. Just as he had somehow fit in, learned the language, found some small, quiet girl and after a long strain managed to put his hand under her shirt and experience his first real erection, caused by something other than his own hand. Then came promises and oaths of eternal love, taking their first real photos together, and exchanging addresses.

And then packing again, saying goodbye to needless things, measuring what was more important to bring and what wasn't. And her tears at the airport and his chin quivering and him holding back from crying as well. Then long waving goodbyes and the plane flight, which lasted an eternity.

All in all, a real kid drama about which an entire album for some boyband could be coolly written.

In the Big Promise Land, where everything is different, his pretty face and his sport spirit helped him a lot (we all know pretty kids have it easier in life than those less pretty, or, God forbid, different). To be a favorite and popular guy, play basketball for the school team, be white, and have a name that's easily pronounced.

Deny wasn't a stupid or naïve kid. All that vagabondage left a trace on him, he was more mature than the other kids in school, he knew well that there was something else in life and somewhere else. That gave him a slightly serious expression on his face and an insane persistence to do everything perfectly.

Jasmina realized how to educate herself and finally, after a few torturous years and studying between two jobs, she started to proudly, although pretty nervously – and as a result began to go gray – work in her field.

Zoka burned out and in the end made peace with a job as one of many scribblers in a big construction company. In the few free moments he hid away into his world behind a computer screen, throwing out everything around him.

Nothing remained from his and Jaca's youthful passion, and everyone was dedicated to their own issues. The communication was usually about computers and Deny, and sex was never mentioned.

Unaccustomed to the new sped up pace of living, they hadn't realized they were completely estranged.

First Bang

Deny was a perfect combination of Jaca's ambitiousness and Zoka's romantic nature.

A tall, white boy from the Balkans (which are probably somewhere in South America), handsome and a real charmer, was absolutely adored by the girls! He used to write to the shy girl from Germany, but that stopped after a few months, right after a surprise rub with a slightly older chick from a higher grade. She dragged him off into the bathroom at some birthday party, where he didn't know anybody. Without saying much, she unbuckled his pants, and when she lifted her skirt and started taking off her underwear, he thought he was going to burst. His first bang lasted for a whole seven seconds.

She just laughed, a little bit disappointed, said it's going to be better next time, peed, and left.

That night, when he came home, he spent a long time looking at his reflection in the mirror.

XXII

"Zoka, get up… Hey, wake up!"

"Haaaa… whaaaat… mmmm…"

"Get up, how can you just sleep?!"

Zoka woke up (he was pissed!) and jumped out of bed.

"What's happening? Is Deny at home? Are you in pain?"

"He is home… and I am in pain, my soul hurts me, how can you just sleep?! Our marriage is going to shit! I'm bored, I get bored, don't you understand! Work-home-work, we haven't gone anywhere in years and you just sit at that PC, who knows, maybe you are chatting to some minors… you don't give a shit! We haven't fucked in who knows how long, I don't want to, I've become completely cold, God knows, maybe I've forgotten… I'm going crazy from this isolation, these spoiled cunts around us and their superficiality, and don't tell me I haven't tried hanging out with my colleagues from work, you know I'm very social, but sometimes I think that they can't understand half of the things I'm saying to them. Stunned, and me with them!

How come you are not aggravated?! Oh yeah, of course, everything is peachy in your world, you wouldn't even try a bit more, you couldn't care less! How are you able to sleep, I can't… just can't anymore…"

***

It is classic. Jaca was deeply suffering from a lack of attention and orgasm. Such a known fact in all neglected marriages. Now, by some rule, there should appear some hot colleague or neighbor, or she runs into some whacked artist and screws with him the same day, like she is in her twenties. Ah, who knows what women are like? Their whole life they are lusting after some special and wicked guy: writers, musicians and brutes, thugs, adventurists and when they get them, they spend years and years making them regular and boring husbands. She regularly dreamt of some wild sex, always with someone else. Every night some other lover. They were cute, smart, and fearless brats who didn't hesitate to ask for what they wanted. Then, there were some shy childhood crushes of hers, which she ran into by pure accident, and some anonymous guys whose appearances she couldn't remember in the morning.

In her dreams, she was falling in love regularly. In those dreams, she could be as old as she wanted to and to look in a way that she wanted. In the morning, after such a dream, she felt completely new and fresh, fulfilled, and it was worth living for those few seconds. Then she opened her eyes… and reality set in, which was far away from horrible, but it was BORING, so much so that it was painful. And that was her worst punishment. Her ambitiousness was slowly subsiding, she was going to work mechanically, she was smiling mechanically (no one ever got it, because Jaca was the prime example of energy and optimism to everyone).

Standing in front of the mirror and watching her still fit body (with a lot of effort she didn't give in to the bombardment of unhealthy calories served across the pond, and she was trying with all her might not to turn into a blob of fat), hating and loving it at the same time, size 36/38 from a twenty-year-old had changed to a decent 40 (hips a little wider after pregnancy, they never returned to their original shape, although Jaca was obsessed with fitness for a time), a few small, unnoticeable wrinkles under the eyes, a few more prominent ones on the forehead, the consequences of a frowning, overly serious twenty-year-old. Stomach a little relaxed, but still flat, legs somewhat stronger (genetic predisposition), hair always tidy. All in all, a woman in her best years, but lonely. One of those women who, when they grab you, don't let you go. Sucks every bit of energy out of you, but first she lets you do whatever you want. For a little bit. Then she punishes you for every injustice done to her, although you had nothing to do with that. In the end, she usually returns to her husband. If he hasn't already started an affair with some girl who just got out of school. And if they don't break up, till the end of their life they act as nothing has ever happened.

When it comes to Zoka and Jaca, after long discussions where Jaca was usually talking and Zoka didn't know what to say, they agreed that it would be time to go on a vacation. They needed to get some money together, get some days off work (almost impossible to get them over the pond, even unpaid ones), and match it with Deny's school.

The coming "home" trip was happening after almost eight years…

***

Zoka and Jaca avoided contact with "our" people. After a few nuisances for the first few years, they finally decided that it was better like that. A few of "our" people they were friendly with lived pretty far away from them. So, they usually just texted or occasionally phoned, planning the next New Year's Eve party or somebody's upcoming birthday.

"Good old Europe! These people, the further they go away from their country, the crazier they are! Must be all that isolation and distance making a whirl in their head," Zoka said, after one unpleasant encounter of the "third kind" at work. One "compatriot," who has been in America for 20 years, was trying, in his pretty twisted mother tongue, to convince Zoka of some historical facts, but Zoka was completely disconnected when it came to politics.

Zoka and Jaca decided not to give in, even to the strongest waves of nostalgia, and never joined one of the clans. Fortunately, free time was their everlasting problem.

One day, Deny surprised them with a question:

"Erm, what is 'our' language?"

"Hmmm… well, Deny, our language is our language… at school, mom and I were taught Serbo-Croatian or Croat-Serbian, which was divided into some two variants, we used a Bosnian dialect… ah who knows… let me start from the beginning… right now, we are speaking Bosnian, which is not the Bosnian it used to be, the one that was taught in schools in Bosnia at the time. Ours is a kind of archaic, maybe old-fashioned language… this language we are speaking right now has been forgotten, but everyone is still using it… that is the South Slavic language-Bosnian dialect… eh, how did you come up with this question…?!"

***

The day of the trip was coming closer, and Jaca was somehow fucked up. Every now and then she was crying and repeating something stupid, like she just hopes her parents will be still alive when they arrive.

Zoka, who had no close family left, and whose distant relatives had moved away somewhere, was participating less in that euphoria.

Zoka's dad died when he was five. His mom never remarried. She lived for her son and house. When Zoka said, after graduating from technical school, that he would like to go to college in Ljubljana, she almost died.

"My son, why would you go that far away from home, we have a college here too. Why would you fuss with a dormitory when you could sleep here at home in your own bed… How will your mother live without you? Can't you see how sick I am?"

***

He barely defeated the guilt that was strangling him, packed some basic clothing, and left.

Knowing he had to do it once. He couldn't stand the constant noose of worry around his neck, because wherever he went and was late just for 5 minutes, she would be dying of fear. When he finally went on an excursion, after a long time spent convincing her, she didn't sleep for a single night. When he came back, she was sick and pale. She hugged him close to her and was crying from joy like he came home from war.

Every girlfriend Zoka had was a tramp, and he couldn't bring any of them home. He was afraid that his mom would start talking some gibberish. She would get mortally ill each time he went on a date with a girl. The ambulance crew knew them well. Who knows how many times they responded to a call coming from their address?

She passed away on the day when Zoka was taking his finals. During his studies, he came home only a few times. The doctor told him she had a stroke (while the neighborhood was gossiping that she had downed some pills). There were only a few people at the funeral because his mom was neither in touch with family nor the neighbors. There were just a few old friends of his late dad who remembered her as a happy, young lady.

When Jaca saw Zoka in a student café near college, she liked him immediately. He was serious, non-chatty, and handsome. They told her they were from the same town, but she couldn't remember him. She was always in the center of attention. They fell in love that same evening. A perfect example how two opposites can attract each other. Jaca was always in charge and the loudest in the group, one of the girls everyone had an eye on, ambitious and stubborn. His Jaca, surprised him for still being a virgin. She had a tongue sharp as a razor, but in reality, behind the armor, she was tender and romantic.

Her folks didn't know about their relationship for over a year. They went home separately, and that secrecy only made their love stronger…

Zoka realized he was staring at a photo of them from the student days for far too long…

***

"Out of all these fucking airport terminals, A to F, our plane is taking off from terminal F," said Jaca, all stiff from the transoceanic flight.

After an awful nuisance, long lines, waiting for luggage and all the fuck with the German customs in Dusseldorf airport, they came to the terminal F. Planes to Sofia, Skopje, Pristina, Bucharest, and Sarajevo departed from terminal F. They finally had time to have a smoke and a coffee, which cost them a whopping 12 DM per person. Deny looked around stunned, everything was kind of strange to him, all these people with massive bags, kids, old women in old-fashioned dresses, and those younger ones all groomed and dressed in the latest fashion, stumpy men with moustaches in leather jackets and the younger ones, sleazy and grumpy. Faces of immigrants from the lower parts of Europe, all of those people who have been migrating from their countries for centuries in some search for a better future.

And always the same: dragging those big "smuggler" bags around the airport, full of smells from homeland, smoked meat and domestic cigarettes, jars full of diverse content, wrapped in native newspaper, domestic brandy and cheese. And the everlasting fights with serious customs officers, who will never understand why those people are dragging all that stuff across the border, refusing to pay for additional luggage, which was heavier than the allowed weight. Arguments and tears.

"Hey fellow countryman, fuck all their steaks… our smoked meat is the world's finest!"

Zoka, Jaca, and Deny came to Sarajevo two days after their planned arrival date because of the endless transfers in Budapest, Vienna, and Zagreb, caused by the bad weather and irregular flights for countries that are on the other side of the globe.

Finally, home. Gray and foggy, buried in white snow that became genuine white after so many years. Mountains surrounding the city, dark and tall, looked as if they were sleeping. Next morning, they went for a walk in the city, completely dazed and exhausted from lack of sleep, partly due to excitement and partly because of the time difference.

Little Girl in Wonderland

"I'm bad at sleeping! It takes me forever to turn off the lights (each instance of sleep is a bit like dying!) and I'm still scared I'll wake up with a headache… I'm so oddly calm. Astonishing! A little more and we're entering a new decade. Fact. What wars will this century bring!? We travel through our time and, like real tourists, stop at the moments to take a picture. We take a pose, spread our smile… and click. Picture.

We fold the pictures into glass jars, putting stickers with names and dates, we conserve them and fold them into our brain storage. Sometimes driven crazy by everyday life, we stop by our brain storage, open one of the colorful jars, smell it a bit, and close it. But just sometimes, we shove our finger into the jar and taste it. Purely pathetic!"

The Contents
of an Entirely Ordinary
Glass Jar

Autumn. Strangely warm. Full of smells that were carried by the wind. The kids are standing in front of the Old school. The new part hasn't been done yet. Because of prolonged civil works, kids from older classes are relocated to surrounding schools. The new school will have a large gym! The biggest in town! And a big, wide hall with a podium and a piano for school performances. And three floors.

Teaching for the students of the three first classes will remain in the Old school. But it will also be renovated! There is commotion in front of the entrance. The girls are talking and showing off their new schoolbags. The boys are jumping and yelling (they're so annoying!), some are playing "Sandokan" or "tag." The Old school is near the street, cars are passing. The street has no sidewalk. One of the boys, running from the "tagged" one, runs over the street. A car… and… a dull hit. The child's body flies for a few seconds and falls onto the street, a few meters away. The boy's older sister is screaming. People from houses across the street run up to him…

It's the first day of school… there's a smell of fresh rolls from the bakery across the street…

***

Old Vida, from the right entrance of the building, wasn't beloved by any child around. She lived on the second floor and always splashed water on the kids. She cursed at them and always complained about the racket. She lived alone with her three cats who had the same evil eyes as her own. No one ever saw family or guests visiting her, and she never drank coffee with any woman from the neighborhood. The kids soon started to whisper that she was a witch, always frowning and wearing black.

When she would enter the building, all the kids would scatter for a moment, and when she passed, they shouted mockingly:

"Viiida you witch, Vida you old witch!"

She would sometimes go back, curse something at them, half into her own chin, or she would damn their mothers (for raising them that way!). Sometimes she would wait for the situation to quieten down and when the kids forgot about her, she would pour a full pot of water over their heads.

That little war was taking on greater proportions. The kids thought up new small mischiefs (once a little boy from the street broke an entire set of a dozen eggs on her door, and once the kids managed to throw a bunch of rotten fruit onto her balcony), and Vida made more accusations and cusses, so a few of the parents got involved.

"Why did you pour water on my Zorica!? What did the kids do to you?! Go and live on a hill where you came from! You've got no children of your own, so you're bothered by mine!"

"Your little girl is the same blabbermouth as you are! And what about her calling me a witch, huh?! And why did she throw garbage onto my balcony with the rest of those brats!?"

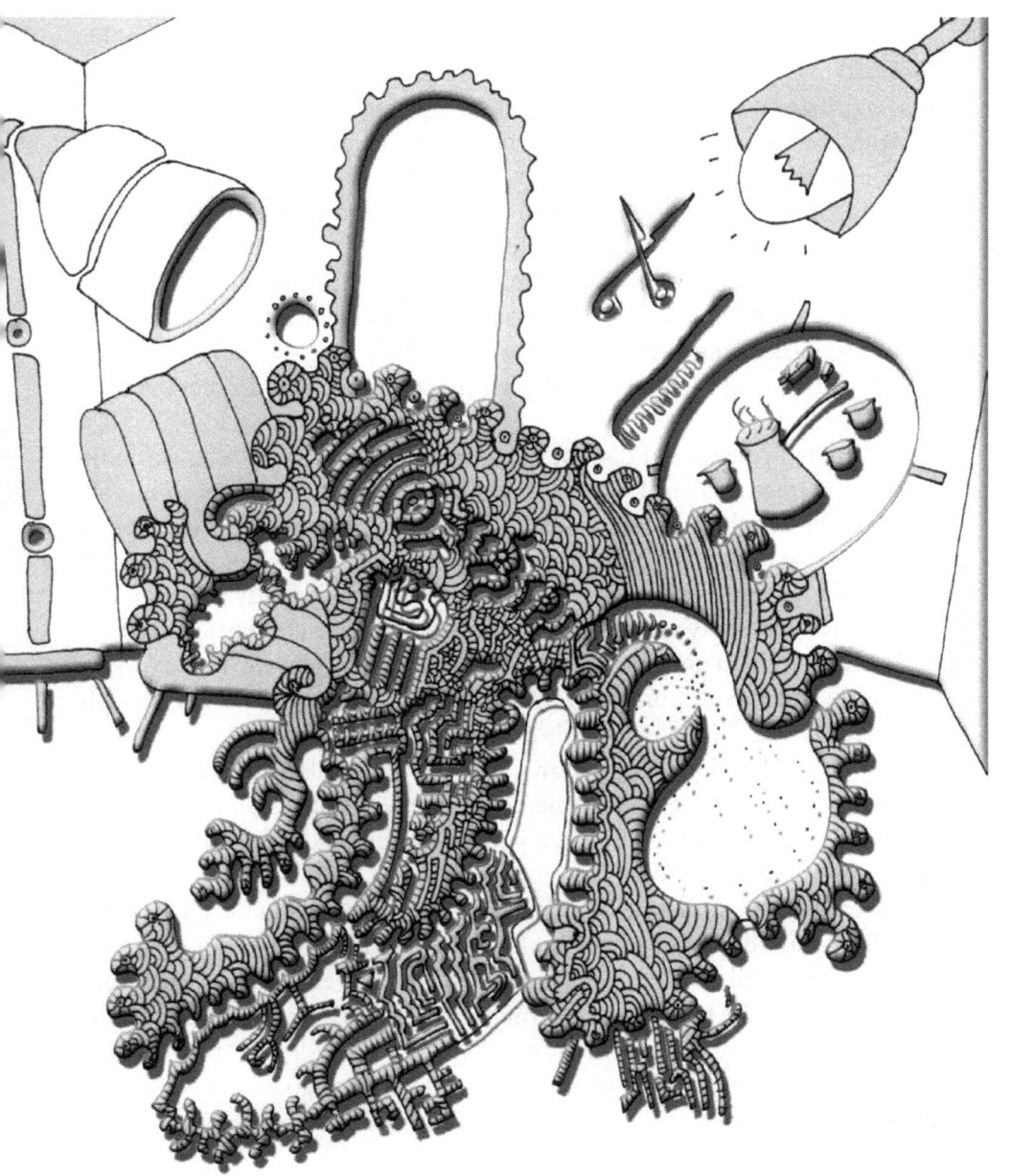

Some parents had differing opinions, so the boy who'd thrown eggs at her door had to apologize to the old lady. His mother was present as well, and he was terrified and with a teary face because of the beating he'd received earlier.

And then slowly, as the children from the street grew up and old Vida got older, everyone somehow forgot or made peace with it. New children didn't play in front of the building but on the new playground across the street, and Vida was still taking care of her cats and rarely went out.

One day, a young family with their two small children moved into her apartment. Aunt Sena (also from the second floor), while being at the hairdresser Nena, heard from the new tenant that the young woman had washed and turned the apartment upside down three times but couldn't get the smell of cats out.

The old lady died at her daughter-in-law and son's place, in a house on the outskirts of town (no one knew she had a son), and it was said that while she was sick, the daughter-in-law took her revenge on everything the old woman had ever done to her. She even poisoned her cats and threw them in the river in front of her eyes. But even on her deathbed, the old lady whispered to her son that his wife was cheating on him and that the children weren't his.

"Ah… there you go, who is born foul, dies foul… you can't do evil your whole life and stay unpunished. Neno, where is Rabija, I hear she brought cheap gold from Turkey… The phone is ringing in the salon."

"Hairdresser's salon "Nena," how can I help you… ah Aida, it's you… yes, you can, yes it's crowded but come in about a half hour… aha… you don't say! Really?! Ah, easy for you when you have a man like that! Okay, see you then, okay, okay… Bye!"

"There you go, someone is born under a lucky star! Aida is going to the seaside again! I don't know… Who knows what that husband of hers does, money doesn't fall from the sky! I know well how every dinar is earned…"

"No darling, the man is an entrepreneur, he has a bakery and a boutique, and now he's opening a café in Travnik!"

"Ah, I'm running a private business too, but I don't go vacationing at the seaside three times a year, maybe I'd go if I found a decent man, but alone with my child and a sick mother… Where will I go?!"

"What happened with that Sutko of yours, last year he didn't leave your salon and brought you flowers and took you out for dinners…"
"Ah Sena, leave it be! Idler and a real drunk! But Nena is holding her own… Men smarter than him have tried to get a hold of Nena's salon and apartment! Without moving his ass! He promised towers and cities… I got burnt one time, my Sena, and never again!"

74   MIMA MIHAJLOVIĆ,

The Chase

The whole town was overrun by street dogs. They rummaged through the garbage, howled through the entire night, they were of all colors and sizes.

We, the kids, would steal pate and "pipi," chicken salami, from home in order to feed them. Every building had its favorites. Ours was Bobi, big, hairy, good-willed flap-ear, always snotty and stinky, but an inviolable boss and the father of Lola, Gara, and Reta's children.

Lola was gray-white-black, small, a bit ugly, with one ear standing upright while the other one was bitten off halfway from some dogfight. She always had offspring! Or was expecting. To Lola's dissatisfaction, Gara appeared from nowhere one night and joined our pack. She was always mad angry.

Because she was the angriest of the bunch, we would always make her chase away our worst enemies – the kids from the yellow building.

Reta was a real beauty. We all deeply believed that she, being ginger with a shiny coat, was a pure breed dog who gave in to street life for her love to Bobby.

When Lola gave birth again, our joy was endless. She let us play with her younglings despite them being little and blind, and we would bring her, a new mother, particularly good food and milk.

One morning, we found Bobi dead next to the river.

"Someone has poisoned him! Probably that old witch! I wish her arm falls off!"

"Maybe he ate something by himself, I saw that they have put rat poison in our basement, and he was in the basement often…"

"You're really stupid! That's impossible, a dog can't die from rat poison, and besides, Bobi was too smart to eat rat poison!"

"Stupid is your mother! Poison is poison…"

"How could you be arguing right now? When Bobby is dead…"

Bobi was buried with a tribute at the same place he was found. In tears, the kids were digging out with sticks a hole big enough for Bobi to fit in.

A month later they were still bringing flowers to his grave, bringing his kids with them.

"See Bobi, these are your children: Ricky, Bobika, Jacky, Sony, and Bella."

One morning, in the old school, news came rushing through: DOG-CATCHERS!

Craziness, panic, fear. The kids were running out of school breathless to hide their pets.

"The manhole from the waterworks, that's a secure place! Or the basement, they surely won't look for them there!"

"Mooooom, pleeeeease," the little girl was screaming, "Let me keep at least one in the house!"

"Don't be crazy, when dad returns from his job, he will throw out you, me and that dog!"

"I know! The old paper factory! That's the place!"

Too late. Executioners, big evil men, had already caught Reta and Lola, and in front of the scared and terrified eyes of the street kids, they choked them with big wires. Afterwards, they threw the lifeless bodies into the truck. They grabbed Ricky, Bobika, and Sony by their legs and threw them against the pavement. The blood stains, as a witness to the terrible crime, remained there for a couple of days.

That night none of the kids were able to sleep. They were crying and screaming in their sleep or waking up with the horrific images flashing in front of their eyes.

Jacky and Bella ran away somewhere. Or at least that is what the kids wanted to believe. Gara's wormy body, or better said the remains, they found only a few days later.

She was buried next to Bobi.

"Mirna, I am going to kill you. How many times have I told you not to play there! You see, just the boys are there!"

Mother Šemsa was relentless. But Mirna was smart. As soon as her old man came home, drunk as usual, she came to him and asked:

"Daaaddy, can I go outside?"

"Yes, child, just go…"

"And I would… I would like to play on the new playground!"

"Mirna! You little brat, what did I tell you!"

"Let the kid play where she wants!"

***

It's not easy to live in a world of spoiled people, accept them and not judge them and even call some of them your friends.

"I am so (once again!) strangely calm."

Astonishing.

Defined emotionally.

Emotionally defined.

Flat.

"In this world of Id you entirely forget about Ego, and especially Superego," thought Little Girl.

"If people aren't directly connected with some tragedy (of which, sadly, there are enough in this crazy world and they happen every day), being directly uninvolved is no excuse, you can't speak of (or, God forbid, think of) antics just like that!"

"All that materialism and media brainwashing, that well thought-out dreadful machinery for control, are no excuse!"

"You can't live like you're alone in the world. It's not easy to see what you're better off not seeing."

"You just get a headache and wonder if it is possible that I am a part of this, too?!"

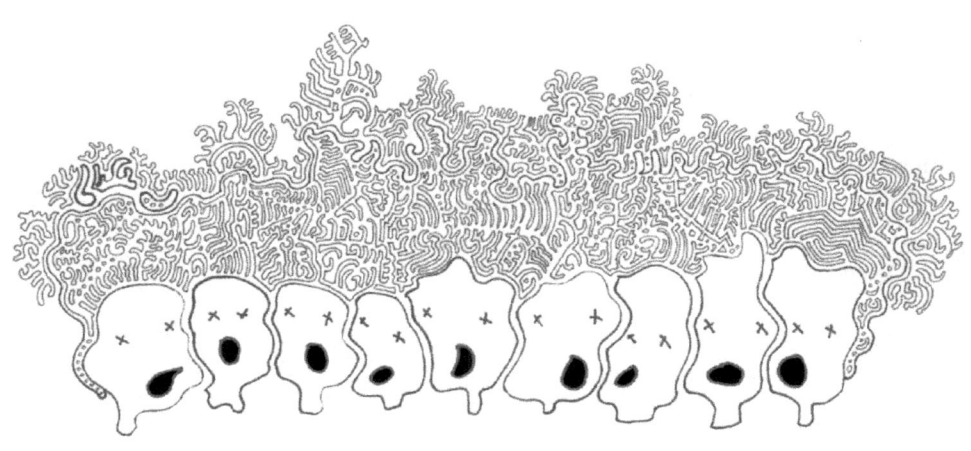

Horror Stories One and Two

I

Little Girl deeply believes that Horror Story No. 2 has never even happened, and she doesn't know how her brain made it all up.

Odd. Too many details (clear as day) erupted out of her guts one morning in The Land of Wonders, as she was packing for the twentieth move in her life. She folded grandma's silverware in newspaper and those two porcelain mugs, an inheritance from her great-grandma Rosaly, Austrian pre-war Volksdeutsche.

She inherited from her that aristocratic, pale, sensitive Germanic tan, her cheekbones, and the behavior of some fucking important duchess.

But it did happen. A Horror Story happened, not very different from a million such women, cliché, war.

A soldier either kills or is killed.

A civilian usually doesn't follow ideals. Just survival. A civilian is either killed or crippled. War is just like that.

A foul thing, it brings to the surface natural molesters, bullies, and killers, who could hardly wait for their five minutes to satisfy some crazy urges and to remain unpunished. A bunch of rotten humanitarian help and expired drugs are sold, someone earns a lot of money, and the majority is usually collateral damage. And I repeat again, psychopaths get their long, long five minutes. Girls are like that thing in Little Red Riding Hood, blah, blah, blah, lost (by refugee bus) in a forest full of evil Wolves who took them out onto a half field with a half wind without Sun. Whether out of shock or shame (the bus full of the remaining Sheep watched the show on the little field without uttering a single word). The girls couldn't do anything besides unflinchingly leave their bodies until the agony passes (if it passes??!) and play with the leaves from the treetops, high, high up, where there's nothing besides the vast green, birds, and clouds. And then the pain started, the shame, the loathing and sickness, which has lasted to this very day. Horror Story...

The smells of repulsive, unfamiliar bodies...

The smells are eternal, no matter how much smoke, speed, or cocaine passes through your nose. Indestructible. Salvation (is it really?) came out of the forest with two shots and some subordinate respective forest pack, who cussed the Wolves' mothers and a hundred Gods, so the Wolves hesitantly returned the Girls into the bus that went on wordlessly.

Totally surreal, like with Bulgakov.

The logic of the story – zero.

Oh, and one of them, angry because of the unfinished business, showing off as the youngest of them, stimulated by the rest and likely high on drugs, perhaps mad out of fear in his frustration, stomped his foot down hard on the Girl's stomach at the end. He was, how ironically, the same age as the Girl.

Well, it all started with that punch. And with those leaves and treetops, high, high up.

Twenty years later, Little Girl (now entirely Big Girl) untwined the thread of the tangled and entirely illogical Horror Story No. 2. She did it first in her body, then in her mind. And all the other Girls, with the same or similar horror stories, know that when the thread is untwined, there's no going back.

You either kill yourself or you live. Very simple. Little Girl (now Big Girl) decided to live out of spite. At least for the time being.

Dictionary of Unfamiliar Words

What is a sheep?

A sheep is an accomplice in crime. If a crime has a witness, but the witness turns his head from the crime, then the sheep is the same as the wolf.

What is a pack?

A pack doesn't have a mind of its own. It has an Alpha who determines everything. If the Alpha is a psychopath, then the pack is pure destruction.

What is a girl?

A girl is meat. Left (if she survives – and she has in this case) to make an individual out of that broken womb. Seemingly she lives a normal life, goes to school, has a boyfriend, listens to music, gets a job, marries and has children (maybe a civilian girl again??!), and she pretends for 20 fucking years that Horror Story No. 2 has never happened.

And it did happen.

Little Girl is left to wonder forever why Horror Story No. 2 had happened to her and didn't happen to, let's say, her sister.

What is trauma?

Trauma is a cancerous group of cells in a human body. Sometimes it grows into a cancer and sometimes not. But it always swims out onto the surface, like some moron when you least need to bother with him.

Moron?

An asshole!!!

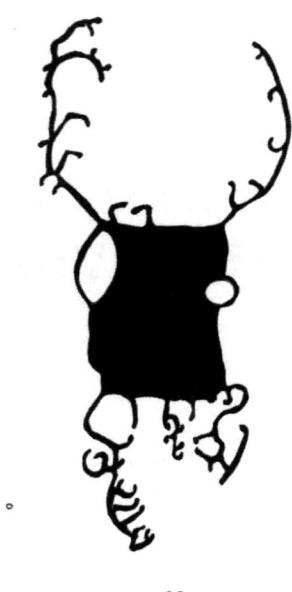

II

Horror Story No. 1 happened a long time ago when Dandy got his name.

No. A child's trust and loyalty mustn't be crippled.

Horror Story No. 1 comes down to the fact that a psychopathic individual cripples a child that has been paralyzed by the trust and closeness it acquired earlier. The child grows, if it's lucky, into a victim.

If it's not, then it grows into that same psychopath. An enchanted circle of horror stories. And there is no forgiveness. Forgiveness is for noble people. And to be a noble man is an art. Little Girl (now Big Girl) has been dealing with forgiveness hard and for a long time. She took into consideration all of the arguments against it. In the end, the only smart thing she realized was that Horror Story No. 1, in some scary, cruel way prepared her for Horror Story No. 2, revealing to her the glimmering world, which educated psychologists would call – Dissociation. As the folk would say, you come out of yourself, and you're fine.

Up until that moment the thread starts to untwine, and you barf up the horror stories. And everything stinks like flowers never even existed. Disgusting.

HORROR STORIES ONE AND TWO ARE ORDINARY STORIES OF ORDINARY GIRLS.

EVERY SIMILARITY WITH REAL PEOPLE IS INTENTIONAL.

XXIV

"This crazy folk hasn't had enough of war, but they are driving now as they are mad!"

"Zoka, look at this! He started overtaking both me and the bus with that wreck of a car, and on top of that, all in a full lane!"

"Ah, you can't find this anywhere else, only in Bosnia!"

Adi lit another cigarette and tossed the box to Zoka.

"What do you say, brother, after so many years… ha? How does this look to you? Bad, isn't it? People just can't wake up, no money, no job, and no will. There, all of us want to go abroad and all of you want to come back, ha, ha, ha, what irony! Not even God can please our people, we always want someone else to take care of our problems. And we love to complain, it's astonishing. Look at my wife, for example. When the war started, all she wanted to do was to get out of here! I broke my back pulling connections and getting the papers, sent her and the kids off while I spent two fucking years here. Finally, I left the country just about when she started to complain how she wanted to go back. Again, I got all of our belongings, bought a car, so I have a place to stuff all that, and we came back. Now she just talks about how dirty it is here, how Germans are smarter than we are, how primitive our people are and so on… Ah, Zoka, my man, who can please women!?"

"But are you fucking someone, you know, someone on the side? I've heard American girls are worthless pussies… What about black girls, have you ever honestly banged a black one? They must be good! I saw on satellite television that MTV crap… ah, they're really good!"

Zoka just threw on a drunken smile and shrugged his shoulders. His wife was going to kill him!

He hadn't been sober for two days already. A few drinks with the in-laws, then he ran into his pals and there you go! Now this crazy Adi managed to convince him to go to a bar in another town.

Like there isn't any beer here! Ah, everyone knows him in this town! So, he is saying he can't even have a drink or grope without the whole town talking about it the next day.

"Thank God, everyone in Bosnia has some sort of car now, so you can go whoring about with decency!"

***

Jaca was walking the streets, holding her mother under the arm.

Rabija was talking extensively, who and what and with whom, like you're reading the gossip section.

Jaca was pretending to listen, while really, she was looking around, noticing changes or those things that had remained the same, searching with her gaze for familiar faces and the stories that go along with them.

"And where has Zoran gone again? This morning he went to get cigarettes and he still hasn't returned," said Rabija, as if accidentally, and turned toward Jaca, observing her reaction.

"Ah, he went off with a friend to Sarajevo," said Jaca, as if carelessly and calmly, but in reality she didn't know whether to worry or be angry.

"Well, will he, for God's sake, be coming home for dinner? You know I've made breaded steak just for him!"

"Oh, mom please, he will come, don't trouble me with this now!"

"I swear to God, Jaco, my child, I don't know… if I were you, I would consider this… it's not right how he's always roaming about…"

"Oh, you always make an elephant out of a fly! It's his vacation as well as mine. And I don't intend to go with him everywhere, I have my own business."

"Well, kids, I don't agree with you! His job is to be with you and the child, and not… How do you two live that way? Is that considered normal in America?"

Jaca only rolled her eyes, then changed the subject:

"We could go to Nena for a hairdo. My hair is all cracked, probably because of that water there and I can't seem to get my hair cut the way I'd like…"

"Well, we might go! That is, to be frank, my only luxury! See how everything is expensive…"

"Mom, I told you to always tell me if you need more money. Please, don't live sparingly if you don't have to!"

Nena, the hairdresser, she hadn't seen for years. Besides the few wrinkles around her eyes and a few bad teeth, she hasn't changed at all. She was still smoking one cigarette after the other and smiled cheerfully.

"Jaco, is that you?! Look at her, a real American! So, how are you?"

"We arrived at last! It's very difficult to get a vacation over there. We barely figured something out…"

"I saw your Dany this morning. God, a real man! Come in! Rabija, how are you? How's you back…? Alma, put the kettle on for coffee and go across the street to Mirso's shop, buy sugar lumps. Tell him to give you the ones I like, he'll know… and bring me two more packs of cigarettes…"

"So Jaca, tell me, what's up in America? I can imagine there's surely everything. What are the hairdressers like? When I saw your hair, I'd say they are really bad! For God's sake, when was the last time you had a haircut?!"

"Oh, Nena, it's been a year and it's a lot easier for me like this. I tie a ponytail and that's it… over there no one has ever cut my hair like you have! A lot of talk, they wind something up, they blow dry you. Then you wash your hair once and nothing is left! No hairdo in sight. I just couldn't be bothered to look for a good hairdresser. I dye my hair myself and that's it…"

"Alma, dear child, is the coffee done? Where is she…? Oh, she hasn't even returned from Mirso yet! See that, dear Rabija, these students aren't what they used to be! Can't even wash the clients' hair, not to mention something else! It's today's youth, my dear, they don't want to do anything! All so sluggish, my God! Ah no wonder. Real war generation. Fucked in the head. They haven't gone anywhere, nor could they, as they have no money. See, my little Alma, she's a refugee child. Her father disappeared and her mother was left with four of them. And, poor her, she's hoping that she will find her husband somewhere. Day in and day out she goes to different organizations

in the hope of hearing something about her husband. And the kids… all sorrow and misery! I told her to send the girl to study the trade at my place…"

"Boss, Mirso says he doesn't have the sort of sugar lump you like. He gave me this one. He says it's also good."

"Alright, c'mon… put the kettle on."

"There you go, like a new person! Hold on, let me put some hair spray on… there you are…"

"Nena, great job! You've brought my mood up a hundred percent! Mom, what do you say?"

"Oh, it's great, really. I don't even know why you let your hair grow, you know yourself it's better short!"

"And Nena, what do you say about me, maybe I could change something?"

"Well, you know, my dear Rabija, I could lighten your hair tone up a bit, the gray hairs will be less visible, and man, that red color, you've had it on forever! You never want anything else! Jaca, you tell her, for God's sake, a few highlights would look good on her?!"

"Oh, try it, mom, it's easy to go back to red if you want to…"

XXV

"My Little Girl, it's pointless but you always laugh! I can see in your eyes that you are bored…"

"A man always finds it difficult in the GRAY WORLD. And if everything is okay, then you make up some other thing to bother you…"

***

Of all the things in the world, Little Girl hated three human traits most of all: being spoiled, lazy, and selfish.

And perhaps for that very reason, she has always been surrounded by bearers of those traits.

No, it has nothing to do with tolerance – in the gray world that is quite dominant!

Everything once again spins around that classic story about the Spaniards or the Portuguese, with how the Portuguese eventually learn Spanish, but the other way round has never happened!

And of course, again, that classical pathetic fate of the Portuguese in Spain. Nothing else but a fucking foreigner. And that Portuguese man badly wishes to change the world as if it were some ordinary thing!

Ah, it's not quite that simple. If you wish to change the world, you shouldn't stay an eternal immigrant. Release your roots (even the fake ones) and then make changes as much as you want! Take on the knowledge of Spanish history, language, culture, and customs, then lightly turn on your brain, receiving generally accepted Spanish certificates, immersing yourself into the contents of everyday Spanish life, and then turn the world upside down. Instead of doing something before thinking.

Those are all of the things that Little Girl had long ago managed, but men… she can't seem to figure out. Just when she thought she'd figured out all the plays and tricks, manipulations, fears and what not, in the end, it would turn out that in certain situations she hadn't learned the basic things.

And to a very stubborn and vain person, such as she was, that made no sense. Ah, how many rises and falls still to go!? Only God knows. And from the start again.

"I once knew a nit of a man. Once…"

God, he was speaking so slowly, every word was like a needle poking into my brain. He could have bought everything for money and power. And still, that almost childlike smile, mostly in the morning, and the words:

"Relax. Tomorrow is another day."

I once knew a nit of a man, a player without balls, a pussy.

Once.

He was so confident.

No, I didn't love him.

Maybe a little, after all…

Little Girl closed the book, switched off the lamp beside her bed, and pulled the sheet over her head.

Good night!

A Letter

I swallow my spit again, smelling my sky and listening to your voice.

A simply green dream and however long it lasts, I don't care. There is nothing you can do about it.

Why have you trampled everything with that damned military boot?! You can't put me into a box, I'm not the Little Prince's sheep.

I am no longer afraid. I know now who I am and how far I can go.

Darling, this waiting is breaking me. The hours are so slow! You think that isn't a box.

Well it is! A filled hole in gray cardboard. You don't hear me, you don't see me, I want to scream!

No, I will simply leave.

And you see, everything I do is irritatingly normal.

Why must I do it first, why must I be the first to touch?

You set this fucking boundary, so I feel like a child doing a forbidden thing.

We no longer want each other at the same time, we don't want each other in the same way. You're far away, and I am no longer happy when you enter the room.

I am irritated when you watch TV or when you talk on the phone.

I'm tired of your standard mechanical questions, mechanical emptying of the ashtray, happening at the exact moment when I wish to put out my cigarette. You're no longer holding my hand while you're sleeping.

You're far away. I'm tired of explaining each of my thoughts, stupid discussions, and apologies.

Lead me, take me away, take me, touch me, break me or bite me, scratch me, wake me up or, best of all, give me enough room to be...

With this fear of myself, I'm probably trapping you...

I'm putting a million kaleidoscope pieces into your head.

And there, on the other side of the glass, New Year is coming, time passes, children dance on the ice...

To my great surprise, you asked me last night: "What is complete happiness?!"

And I didn't know how to explain it to you. I said: *"I will know when I feel it."*

Forgive me, I didn't mean to hurt you. It is likely that we are that complete happiness, and I will find that out sometime after, some other day. My interim feelings are now great and I live someone else's life (I've already told you that) and I will live my life another time. Why do you take up that defensive attitude as if you're fighting for some truth so frantically?! Aren't our truths the same?

I think they are, perhaps just a bit differently defined.

And are you afraid of me or for me? Tell me which exactly?!

For me? Don't worry.

I'm just a little bit crazy, but it's just sometimes and on the outside. And on the inside, you can't see it anyway. Don't worry, I am not Betty Blue. That was just the movie. Reality is happening now, in this moment, when you enter the house and I'm watching you and studying each change on your face.

Please, let me enter your life at last. Let me stroll in freely, like a friend into a lover's dream.

Don't push me with the grimaces on your face! And again, waiting, and everything starts over again, and the fatigue is getting stronger, and it shamelessly overtakes me like an ordinary thing.

And another night passes. Another euphoria. And another thirst. It's still dark, and we're laughing…

***

Once upon a time, T. and Little Girl had a Little Story. Now, after so many years, when both of them are the main characters in some entirely new stories in entirely different ends of the world, maybe sometimes, just sometimes, they think about that Little Story at the same time.

Maybe sometimes, when some entirely accidental detail from their present lives reminds them of it.

XXVI

"Ugh, how I hate this cold! Well, it doesn't have anything to do with the weather, rather… it's… like it comes from inside… I'm probably alone again…"

This little thought passed through Little Girl's head as she was heading into the cold winter wind.

And Again,
Little Girl's Little Story

For a long time, I hadn't been aware of the finality of life and the eternity of a moment.

Today, I spotted in the mirror the eyes of one old, stubborn soul. I was almost frightened!

I don't know why I think of you so often.

Sometimes it irritates me and sometimes it soothes me, then it frightens me again.

This summer I wanted to tell you so much, but you've known it all for a long time.

Have a rest and forgive me.

And it really hurts me that we didn't have time to share some simple, tiny joy…

***

Every month is the same thing. Sometimes a bit stronger, sometimes weaker, but usually the same.

A mix of hormones, current moods, and aches, which even the devil has become tired of.

First easy, dull and insidious, and then it gets stronger and stops pretending, and then, it starts to march freely and extremely provocatively.

Soon after that, it goes frantically on a healthy mind, it gets a shape, smell, color, and a face. Even the temperature.

Every Pain is a temptation.

Can I take it, can I take it… can I take it… can I… take it…

And when you think that you can't take it anymore, then it suddenly starts to hurt even more, and more, and more, and it breaks you entirely.

And you become some spongy substance.

And every Pain is the same. Evil, insidious, disarming, humiliating.

And I would be lying if I said I didn't envy people who don't have to fight with Pain.

Any kind.

On the sixth day of the visit to his hometown, Dany ended up in the emergency room for stomach pumping. He'd gotten wasted on brandy with some pals and was barely alive. Zoka and Jaca spent the night beside his bed, crying wordlessly.

But everything ended well.

The day after, probably due to some crazy game of mixed feelings and memories, Jaca remembered her first time getting drunk with the girls from her class. It was caused by some cheap menthol-liquor in the first year of Gymnasium during the celebration of New Year's Eve.

She recollected how they screamed when Sanja's sister appeared at the door at some later hour with Davor, who was player number 1 in the Gymnasium and beyond.

The five of them: Sanja, Jaca, Amra, Dragana, and Duca.

Dead wasted at Sanja's apartment for New Year's Eve.

Sanja's family were staying with their relatives in the countryside. Maja (Sanja's elder sister) celebrated New Year's Eve with her friends at some guy's place in the building across the street. So she came to check on her younger sister, and with Davor!

Who knows where those people are now…

She still keeps in contact via mail with Sanja and Duca. One is in Switzerland and the other in Italy. Amra got lost somewhere during the war going around humanitarian organizations and who knows where she is now or what she does. She'd always been ambitious!

And about Dragana, all she knows is that she's living somewhere in Montenegro, still with her folks, studying in college who knows for how long now and she is still alone (as always).

And Davor? Davor is in Holland.

There, everyone's gone their own way.

"I should do something about the celebration of prom anniversary. No one has organized anything yet…"

"Everyone's busy with their own problems."

Then came the day of return. Jaca, Zoka, and Dany packed heavy-handedly, all three of them nervous because of the trip, pushed their suitcases into the neighbor's car, and started toward the airport…

Jaca had barely convinced her folks not to follow her to the airport. Rabija had been crying since early in the morning.

And only when their neighbor, Bruno, had said there was no way everyone would fit into the car (which had been more than obvious), she had given up.

"Mom, it's enough, we didn't die!"

"Oh, my child, who knows when we'll see each other again..."

"Well, we'll see each other, it's not that far away... look, now you've made me cry too..."

The entire neighborhood had marched through their house that morning, including the family.

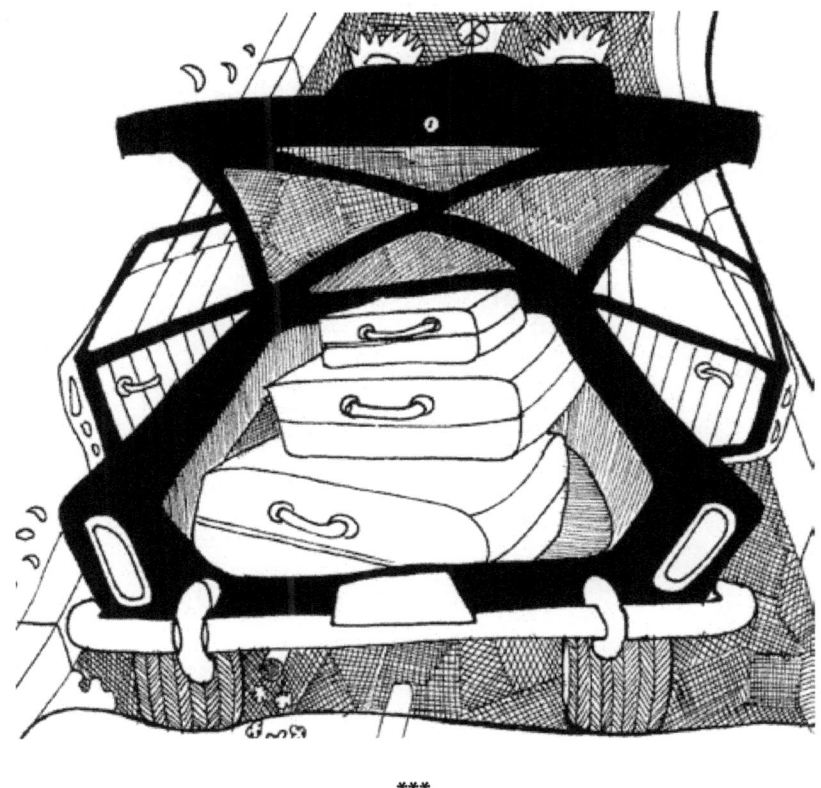

***

The moment the plane's engine started, preparing for take-off, Zoka and Jaca felt a kind of relief, as well as an enormous emptiness in their stomachs.

They barely spoke to each other until the end of the summer...

Heroes of
the Ordinary Stories

Ordinary people from ordinary stories normally look alike.
  And if they think they will be excluded for that, they are wrong.
  Every similarity with real characters is entirely intentional.

Earthly
Constants

The presence of earthly constants in these stories is also intentional.
The balance of emotions (if there is any) is accidental.

Final Word

Every truth is an entirely relative thing.

It normally depends on the angle from which it is observed as well as the observer themselves.

And if the observer is, by some case, the participant (as it usually is), then the truth gets another dimension.

Which means that subjectivity is guaranteed?

Actually we are all participants. There are no observers.

(And even YOU – who, for the purpose of entertainment, reclining somewhere in the comfort of your armchair or in the intimacy of your bathroom, sitting on the toilet and reading this easy-going material – not even you are certain. There, you have stepped into this Final word almost up to your knees.)

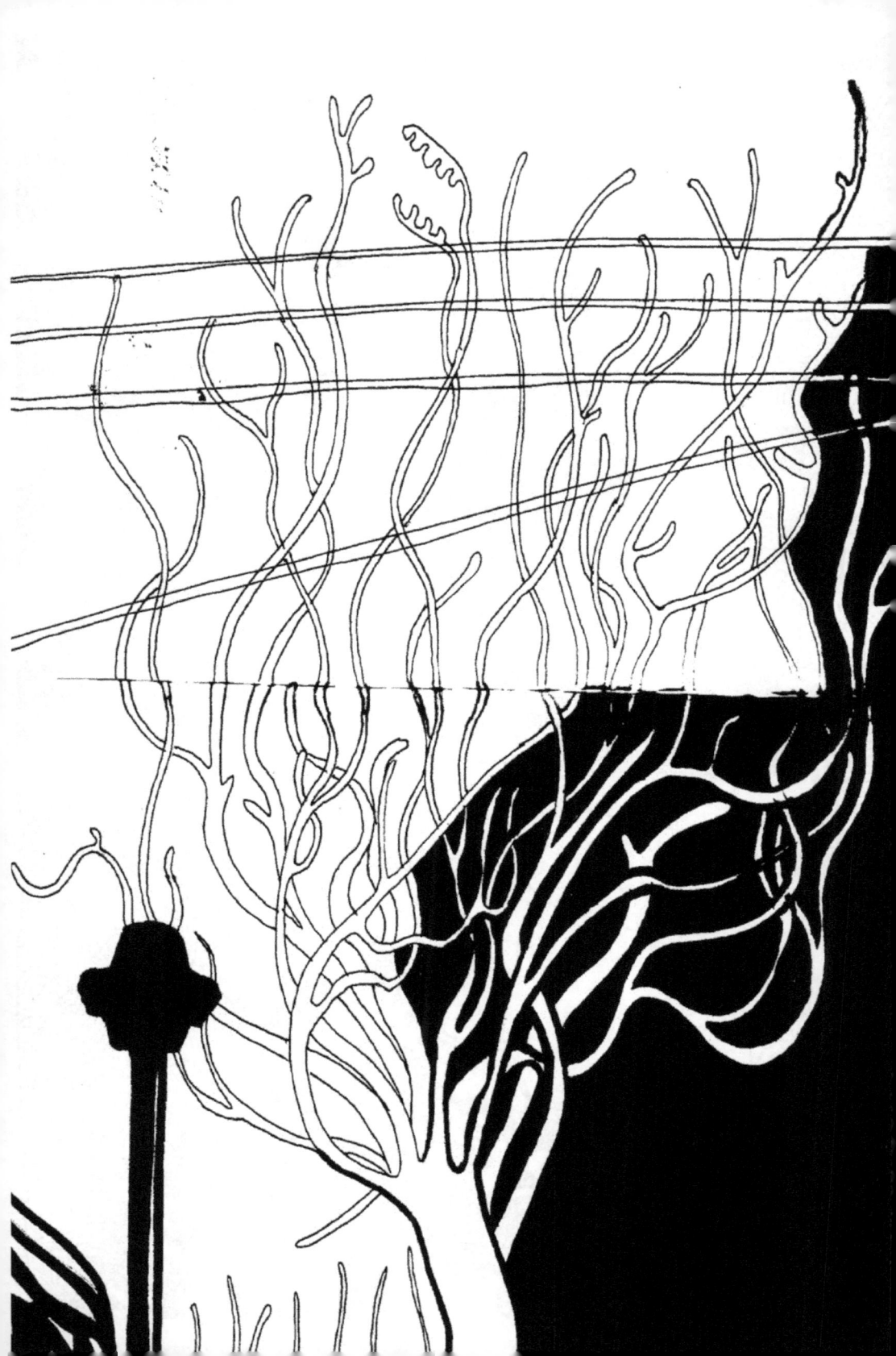

Afterword

Mima Mihajlović's *Everyday Stories*

Art forms were once guided by a steady stream, precisely established. That's how a novella became defined as concise storytelling, which most often contains just one event of an individual human's fate in a relatively short time span and a limited field. Unlike a novella, a novel could always get the basis of life, and to no end, flow like a torrent carrying everything that falls into its flow. And what is today's current literature but marketable theatre of imagination and a battlefield of all passions, and even sanctuary of all laziness.

Mima Mihajlovic has, in the very title of her writing, determined through the plural form that it is actually about multiple stories, the meanings of which are not always uniform, nor are they constantly, firmly connected or encapsulated separately. "Turnip Without a Root" (Repa bez korijena) and "The Chase" (Hajka) could function independently (although Titoslav thinks about "Turnip…"), but the whole text is not structured in such a way that we could say whether it is a novella or a story. It would be better to call this text a postmodern novel, which we could continue to weave, but the author has purposefully left us with options to finish the needlework by our own choice.

The composition of the piece is without strict regulation or plan, without being focused just on one action, to doubtlessly create one effect. The means of expressions, words, and literary ornaments, were used functionally. Mima's storytelling is extraordinary. She reduces some actions, saves them, summarizes, synthesizes, and slices them with a sharp tongue, in a moment with jargon, a cuss, then again with an artistic description followed by a powerful and big breath of life. Her style is characterized by irony followed by ingenious black and white illustrations. Writing like this is actually a world in itself, and it is a mirror of the absurdity of existence, which still neither subjugates nor underestimates the turn of a situation in an often-narrow impersonal space, like hope in some new day.

Everyday Stories begin with Titoslav and continue with Dandy. In British English, the term "dandy" has a derogatory meaning, as a man who is obsessively focused on his looks, or a toff, coxcomb, fop. The other meaning is colloquial in American English, and means "great, nice, handsome," and that word can signify some excellence in its class. You could say there is a fine line between excellence and being a toff, but that solely depends on a person's style, aesthetic and motivation, and of course on personal views, tastes of other people, and the surroundings. As a curiosity, "dandy" is actually registered as a profession in Castro's Cuba.

Titoslav mostly goes by the name Tisi, Tile, most often with a capital letter of the name and a full stop, as T., which associates with Kafka's hero from *The Trial* (Josef K. or just K.). T. either is not a real *dandy*, considering the meanings, or is only partially, fragmented in pictures. He is "an eternal boy" ("Tisi was 28 years old and had a good working record as a train dispatcher. And an eternal boy…"[1]). At times he feels forgotten, "completely and hopelessly trapped in the past," and then "enjoying his masochistic Goethe's acts on a daily basis."[2]

At times, *Everyday Stories* by Mirna Mihajlović can be associated with the famous *Exercises in Style* by Raymond Queneau, which are just ordinary happenings from everyday life, but are given with a lot of humor and irony, thus, exploring language and the objective relativity of linguistic signs, as well as the folk surroundings. That is why such texts can be considered truly lingual and even a form of cultural laboratory.

No, he just looked speechlessly into an imaginary dot.
No, cramping up from pain and screaming.
No! Still looking at the dot.
No, no! Screaming and cramping up inside of himself, but in reality, he was quiet and speechlessly looking into the same imaginary dot.[3]

Much like Kafka's K., Mima's T. has certain cognition, but not enough to develop his own personality.

....

[1]   Mirna Mihajlović, *Everyday Stories*, p. 10.
[2]   Ibid., p. 13.
[3]   Ibid., p. 13.

To have a bit of an overview of this story, Dandy gets a big introduction in this title. T. and Dandy are actually one unbreakable symbiotic unity, but in this case – two parasites who alternate the roles.

Some friends of T. claim that Dandy appeared in T.'s life on one sad day, when our main character got his first undeserved slap from his drunk father, and his mother shoved his first Prozac down his throat, because T.'s mother, in her kind primitive head, didn't know how to calm down the hysterical crying of a surprised child.

Actually, then, T. opened the door to Dandy and let him into his life.[4]

Meanings are partial and molecular. No excess in terms of wholeness. That poetic procedure is, actually, adapted fragmentation of the image of the modern world, achieved with hallucinatory blinks and road darkened by their incompleteness, reduced notice, realized by the absence of logical connection between the images. He evolved, he changed…

"T. and Dandy are actually one unbreakable symbiotic unity, but in this case – two parasites who alternate the roles."[5]

What follows is the confrontation between Fear and Dandy, and Tisi's philosophizing and daydreaming, in the story "Clothes," in which he remembers waiting for Boby:

No! He looked bewildered, with hangdog eyes, a real cowardly pussy one, and he was breathing with a half-open, wet mouth.
NO! NO! NO!
He is not going!!!
The end. And it hasn't even started yet.
It was a sign of an everlasting capitulation of one's youth, and so little was needed, so little…[6]

So, *Everyday Stories* are not built on the absolute acknowledgment of a breakdown. In this text there is a significant number of parts constituted by the principle of vortex composition, where the reader does not have a feeling of previously thought-out creation, but rather, the work resembles a movement initiated by resignation in which one picture, one moment, by association, calls on the following one, the next one, which potentiates base

....

[4]   Ibid., p. 18.
[5]   Ibid., p. 18.
[6]   Ibid., p. 25.

emotion and intonation, and in its essence holds liable coherency (which the entire "Little Story" testifies to).

You could say that the most accomplished parts in the book *Everyday Stories* are exactly the ones which are similar to the techniques of the stream of consciousness, when the hero's time becomes completely subjective and in a typical film-like fashion carries a fast sequence of images, one over the other:

> My Little Girl used to say that we love only once and usually tragically, and the rest are just surrogates of that first, tragic love. Personally, I never agreed with that. My Little Girl had always been a little pathetic anyway. "And I say again… there is no more God… until the next moment…"[7]

Ostensible release is present in many places and it is carried out as a leitmotif (see, for instance, "Turnip Without a Root"). The author interestingly introduces rhymes and a few slogans, which demystify fragments of loneliness. Out of nowhere, as if Charles Bukovski himself had burst out of her, she begins to sing during the narration, thus activating the effect of wonder.

Mima Mihajlovic also shows us that she knows how to intensify a distinct modern understanding of the world, using (when it is least expected!) a structure of a comic, achieving the aforementioned effect of wonder:

> "Ay, ay, Corto Maltese, did you have to show up in this comic?! Can't you see there aren't any pictures in it, just a lot of stupid exclamation marks! Without screams!"
> Dandy laughed, spat out a booger from the bottom of his lungs, and thought that there wasn't even a trace of femininity in him! Right afterwards, he pulled a white piece of chalk out of his pocket. He drew a hopscotch, then instead of numbers he only drew nines. And just like that, he started jumping in his socks and mumbling the nursery rhyme:

Nothing with anything x 9

Head in the bag x 9

Final word x 9

And full stop x 9

---

[7]   Ibid., p. 26.

Bad legs x 9

Steady pace x 9

072 x 9

No regrets x 9

With a line x 9

Slow game x 9

Quick rhythm x 9

Conformity x 9... I want to slide...

Bing! Bang! Bang! And Dandy ended up in a dumpster with withered flowers on his head and a piece of apple between his teeth. He got up, dusted himself off, laughed happily like a child, and left.[8]

Mima actually does not want to revive the past evocatively and pathetically, but she ironizes disordered fairy-like systems by filling them with context full of current chaos and entropy. The example of that is visible in the story "Pseudo Dandy."

"Little Story No. 2" appears, at first, as a new cycle, that is until it comes to the Roman numeral sixteen (XVI). The text is divided by stars, Roman numerals (XXVI total) and story titles, but numbers follow one another, regardless of a new narrative, i.e., a new story.

Some writing critics (and to repeat: this text would best fit the postmodern, that is, the poststructural novel, so called *new readings*[9]) consider the heroes as carriers and interpreters of the writer's attitude, understanding, and ideas, that attract the reader's main attention. Their actions, behavior, understanding, thoughts, emotions, and character must be portrayed in such a way that the characters appear lifelike and believable, characteristic and representative of a given epoch, society, class, or state of human con-

....

[8]   Ibid., pp. 37-38.

[9]   Zdenko Lešić, *New Readings, Poststructuralist Reading* (Sarajevo: Buybook, 2003); Wolfgang Iser, *A Companion* (Walter de Gruyter, 2012), pp. 225, 257.

sciousness. To achieve that, the writer has to have special abilities – a highly developed gift of observation, perception, selection, and generalization, the strength of imagining and experiencing, and a very strong talent for forming images of life and people, so that such perceptions and experience enable her to paint images of spiritual life and mentality of her heroes.[10]

Our author multiplies herself in her creative sense, with which she reaches objectivity and liveliness while showing the events and heroes. Besides that, in the application of the art process she creates a personal vision-like world, without diminishing the cultural reality: on the contrary, in the essence of her thought always exists one truth which Mima Mihajlović believes in and it is the incentive, in her view, of reality, as well as life. On the basis of this, she can create her "own world," presented in such a way that it artistically brings life ("Game," "Day Before," "Day After," "Little Girl in Wonderland").

Basically, "Tisi didn't jump from the bridge, and Little Girl didn't come to her hometown for six years."[11]

From page 59, T. or Tisi or Titoslav disappears, and Deny appears: "Because we've lost our main hero in the mass of entirely ordinary stories, it's time to move onto other similar stories. Just for variety's sake. Little Deny, Titoslav's neighbor from the other entrance of the same building, was a youngster when the shit started." We meet his parents, Jasmin/Jaca (who "was deeply suffering from a lack of attention and orgasm"[12]) and Zoran/Zoka ("serious, non-chatty, and handsome"[13] who "burned out and in the end made peace with a job as one of many scribblers in a big construction company"[14]).

War, Bosnia, and the Bosnian theme are the inspirational connection which Mima often and affirmatively writes about, sometimes critically, but always with unhidden feelings ("First Bang"). Her open-mindedness is, above all, in her desire for goodness and humanity towards all people and her reflections are of a deep, intellectual sensibility. Therefore, they are pro-

....

[10] This cannot be taken literally, because the key to the interpretation of a literary work should not always be sought in the writer's biography (which was well explained by French literary theorist Roland Barthes in the essay "Death of the Author," 1968, emphasizing the meaning and activity of the recipient).

[11] Ibid., p. 56.

[12] Ibid., p. 64.

[13] Ibid., p. 67.

[14] Ibid., p. 62.

moting principles of tolerance and civilized dialogue and, among other things, they refer to interculturalism as a Bosnian destiny.

"Little Girl in Wonderland" is a brief record in which Little Girl wakes up after a bad night's sleep and announces the next story ("The Contents of an Entirely Ordinary Glass Jar"):

> We fold the pictures into glass jars, putting stickers with names and dates, we conserve them and fold them into our brain storage. Sometimes driven crazy by everyday life, we stop by our brain storage, open one of the colorful jars, smell it a bit, and close it. But just sometimes, we shove our finger into the jar and taste it. Purely pathetic![15]

"The Chase" is written in plural, intertwining first and third person. "New Playground" is a short picture from childhood, after which Little Girl enters her "Horror Stories One and Two."

Mima's work is a literary type that provides a range of knowledge about life and the world, and has both educational and social significance ("Dictionary of Unfamiliar Words"): what is a sheep? a pack? a girl?

> HORROR STORIES ONE AND TWO ARE ORDINARY STORIES OF ORDINARY GIRLS.
> EVERY SIMILARITY WITH REAL PEOPLE IS INTENTIONAL.[16]

Like a comic strip, it is moving again through narration of (dis)connected sights ("Letter," "And Again, Little Girl's Little Story").

> *"Relax. Tomorrow is another day."*
> I once knew a nit of a man, a player without balls, a pussy.
> Once.
> He was so confident.
> No, I didn't love him.
> Maybe a little, after all…
> Little Girl closed the book, switched off the lamp beside her bed, and pulled the sheet over her head.
> Good night![17]

....

[15] Ibid., p. 70.

[16] Ibid., p. 82.

[17] Ibid., p. 87.

(Pulling the bed sheets over one's head was seen in the earlier stories with Tisi, in which he describes himself in the same way before going to bed.)

———

I swallow my spit again, smelling my sky and listening to your voice.
A simply green dream and however long it lasts, I don't care. There is nothing you can do about it.
Why have you trampled everything with that damned military boot?!
You can't put me into a box, I'm not the Little Prince's sheep.
I am no longer afraid. I know now who I am and how far I can go.
Darling, this waiting is breaking me. The hours are so slow! You think that isn't a box.
Well it is! A filled hole in gray cardboard. You don't hear me, you don't see me, I want to scream![18]

———

Once upon a time, T. and Little Girl had a Little Story. Now, after so many years, when both of them are the main characters in some entirely new stories in entirely different ends of the world, maybe sometimes, just sometimes, they think about that Little Story at the same time.
Maybe sometimes, when some entirely accidental detail from their present lives reminds them of it. [19]

Mima will confuse the readers. Is it possible that T. or his alter ego, "Dandy," i.e., the Pseudo Dandy is the character with the military boots… Coming back to the description of Titoslav, we would not say they belong to the same generation… From page 65 onward we are again with Dany, Jaca, and Zoka, who, while leaving Bosnia "felt a kind of relief, as well as an enormous emptiness in their stomachs."[20]

And for the characters of "Ordinary Stories" and "Earthly Constants," together with the form of relief over the text, the author gives us amphibolous philosophical answers in the end, as seen in her "Final Word":

Every truth is an entirely relative thing.

....

[18]   Ibid., p. 88.
[19]   Ibid., p. 90.
[20]   Ibid., p. 93.

MIMA MIHAJLOVIĆ,

It normally depends on the angle from which it is observed as well as the observer themselves.
And if the observer is, by some case, the participant (as it usually is), then the truth gets another dimension.
Which means that subjectivity is guaranteed?
Actually we are all participants. There are no observers.
(And even YOU – who, for the purpose of entertainment, reclining some-where in the comfort of your armchair or in the intimacy of your bath-room, sitting on the toilet and reading this easy-going material – not even you are certain. There, you have stepped into this Final word almost up to your knees.)[21]

Changes are always welcome. The style cannot solely depend on the current aesthetical taste of the society. This unusual text could even cause a revolt among the segregated Bosnian national literature: it deviates from the still prevalent, outdated, "academic" Bosnia-Herzegovina norms, like any other engaged "tribal" / "party" political groups (the ones that do not belong to the Bosnians, Serbs, or Croats… but the "others"!)

We know that the existence of the comic is connected with the appear-ance of mass media, existing, at the beginning, as an additional entertain-ment for the newspaper readers, but soon becoming an independent me-dium, "the ninth art," as well as a medium of the future. According to its abruptness, contour cuts, permitted chaos, and sometimes the carelessness of free expression, this text reads fast, but it also demands the return to cer-tain actions, as well as "landscapes" although Mima Mihajlovic tells the story in a way that holds the reader in, even when something appears redundant, but it is actually in a function of "balance of emotions" of ordinary people from an ordinary story.

Medina Džanbegović

....

[21]   Ibid., p. 96.

About the Author

Mima Mihajlović was born in 1974 in Kollbelmoor, Germany. Until she was eighteen, she lived in Zenica, Yugoslavia. Since 1992 and during the war in her homeland, she moved forcibly and not forcibly twenty-three times around the countries of the former Yugoslavia and the Netherlands. Since 2000 Mima has been living and working in Rotterdam, in the Netherlands. *Everyday Stories* is Mima's first book. In addition to writing, Mima is involved in singing, songwriting, vintage hairstyles, and human rights.

MEBET

by Alexander Grigorenko

Mebet concerns a man of the taiga, a hunter, in a moving narrative that blends ethnographic detail, indigenous mythology, and the snowy landscapes of the Arctic. The protagonist is a Nenets, a member of one of the peoples who call far northern Russia home. Dubbed "The Gods' Favorite" for his seeming imperviousness to harm or grief, Mebet earns the envy and derision of his fellow tribesmen. He lives that carefree and blessed life until his old age, when one day a supernatural messenger arrives to lead him to where the realms of the living and the dead meet. Now the Gods' Favorite must confront the price to be paid for his elevated position, and a series of dread trials that lie in store.

Called a dark and terrifying fantasy and the Nenets *Lord of the Rings* by Russian writer and journalist Sergey Kuznetsov, Grigorenko's *Mebet* is a powerful story about humanity, personal fate, and responsibility. Leading Russian literary critic Galina Yuzefovich welcomed *Mebet* as a true epic for the Nenets, a book that is profound, thrilling and vibrant. Whether the book will earn that lofty place within Nenets culture remains to be seen, but the very publication of the book marks a watershed event.

Buy it > www.glagoslav.com

I Want a Baby and Other Plays

by Sergei Tretyakov

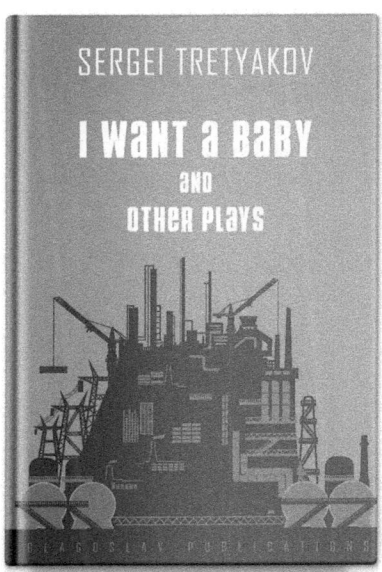

When Sergei Tretyakov's ground-breaking play, *I Want a Baby*, was banned by Stalin's censor in 1927, it was a signal that the radical and innovative theatre of the early Soviet years was to be brought to an end. A glittering, unblinking exploration of the realities of post-revolutionary Soviet life, *I Want a Baby* marks a high point in modernist experimental drama.

Tretyakov's plays are notable for their formal originality and their revolutionary content. *The World Upside Down*, which was staged by Vsevolod Meyerhold in 1923, concerns a failed agrarian revolution. *A Wise Man*, originally directed by the great film director and Tretyakov's friend, Sergei Eisenstein, is a clown show set in the Paris of the émigré White Russians. *Are You Listening, Moscow?!* and *Gas Masks* are 'agit-melodramas', fierce, fast-moving and edgy…

Buy it > www.glagoslav.com

A Brown Man in Russia
Lessons Learned on the Trans-Siberian
by Vijay Menon

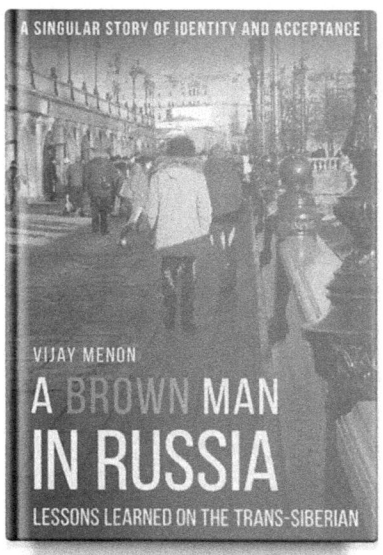

A Brown Man in Russia describes the fantastical travels of a young, colored American traveler as he backpacks across Russia in the middle of winter via the Trans-Siberian. The book is a hybrid between the curmudgeonly travelogues of Paul Theroux and the philosophical works of Robert Pirsig. Styled in the vein of Hofstadter, the author lays out a series of absurd, but true stories followed by a deeper rumination on what they mean and why they matter. Each chapter presents a vivid anecdote from the perspective of the fumbling traveler and concludes with a deeper lesson to be gleaned. For those who recognize the discordant nature of our world in a time ripe for demagoguery and for those who want to make it better, the book is an all too welcome antidote. It explores the current global climate of despair over differences and outputs a very different message – one of hope and shared understanding. At times surreal, at times inappropriate, at times hilarious, and at times deeply human, *A Brown Man in Russia* is a reminder to those who feel marginalized, hopeless, or endlessly divided that harmony is achievable even in the most unlikely of places.

Buy it > www.glagoslav.com

The Door was Open

by Karine Khodikyan

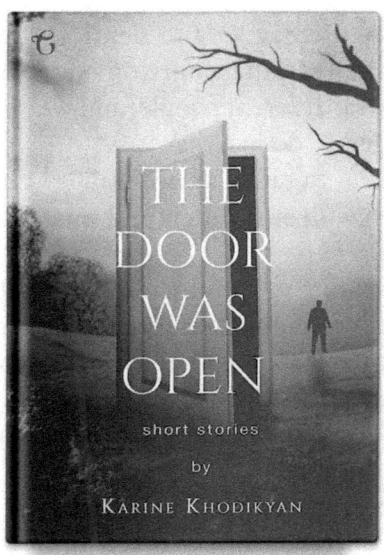

The short fiction of Karine Khodikyan can be described as intellectual fiction for women. These short stories with a "mystical touch" tell stories about women – young and old, happy and sad; even when the protagonist is not a woman, the story will immerse you into the life of a woman, revealing her role in anything and everything.

This book was published with the support of the Ministry of Culture of the Republic of Armenia under the "Armenian Literature in Translation" Program.

Buy it > www.glagoslav.com

Glagoslav Publications Catalogue

- *The Time of Women* by Elena Chizhova
- *Andrei Tarkovsky: The Collector of Dreams* by Layla Alexander-Garrett
- *Andrei Tarkovsky - A Life on the Cross* by Lyudmila Boyadzhieva
- *Sin* by Zakhar Prilepin
- *Hardly Ever Otherwise* by Maria Matios
- *Khatyn* by Ales Adamovich
- *The Lost Button* by Irene Rozdobudko
- *Christened with Crosses* by Eduard Kochergin
- *The Vital Needs of the Dead* by Igor Sakhnovsky
- *The Sarabande of Sara's Band* by Larysa Denysenko
- *A Poet and Bin Laden* by Hamid Ismailov
- *Watching The Russians (Dutch Edition)* by Maria Konyukova
- *Kobzar* by Taras Shevchenko
- *The Stone Bridge* by Alexander Terekhov
- *Moryak* by Lee Mandel
- *King Stakh's Wild Hunt* by Uladzimir Karatkevich
- *The Hawks of Peace* by Dmitry Rogozin
- *Harlequin's Costume* by Leonid Yuzefovich
- *Depeche Mode* by Serhii Zhadan
- *The Grand Slam and other stories (Dutch Edition)*
  by Leonid Andreev
- *METRO 2033 (Dutch Edition)* by Dmitry Glukhovsky
- *METRO 2034 (Dutch Edition)* by Dmitry Glukhovsky
- *A Russian Story* by Eugenia Kononenko
- *Herstories, An Anthology of New Ukrainian Women Prose Writers*
- *The Battle of the Sexes Russian Style* by Nadezhda Ptushkina
- *A Book Without Photographs* by Sergey Shargunov
- *Down Among The Fishes* by Natalka Babina
- *disUNITY by Anatoly Kudryavitsky*
- *Sankya* by Zakhar Prilepin
- *Wolf Messing* by Tatiana Lungin
- *Good Stalin* by Victor Erofeyev
- *Solar Plexus* by Rustam Ibragimbekov

- *The Garden of Divine Songs and Collected Poetry of Hryhory Skovoroda*
- *Adventures in the Slavic Kitchen: A Book of Essays with Recipes*
- *Seven Signs of the Lion by Michael M. Naydan*
- *Forefathers' Eve by Adam Mickiewicz*
- *One-Two by Igor Eliseev*
- *Girls, be Good by Bojan Babić*
- *Time of the Octopus by Anatoly Kucherena*
- *The Grand Harmony by Bohdan Ihor Antonych*
- *The Selected Lyric Poetry Of Maksym Rylsky*
- *The Shining Light by Galymkair Mutanov*
- *The Frontier: 28 Contemporary Ukrainian Poets - An Anthology*
- *Acropolis: The Wawel Plays by Stanisław Wyspiański*
- *Contours of the City by Attyla Mohylny*
- *Conversations Before Silence: The Selected Poetry of Oles Ilchenko*
- *The Secret History of my Sojourn in Russia by Jaroslav Hašek*
- *Mirror Sand: An Anthology of Russian Short Poems*
- *Maybe We're Leaving by Jan Balaban*
- *Death of the Snake Catcher by Ak Welsapar*
- *A Brown Man in Russia by Vijay Menon*
- *Hard Times by Ostap Vyshnia*
- *The Flying Dutchman by Anatoly Kudryavitsky*
- *Nikolai Gumilev's Africa by Nikolai Gumilev*
- *Combustions by Srđan Srdić*
- *The Sonnets by Adam Mickiewicz*
- *Dramatic Works by Zygmunt Krasiński*
- *Four Plays by Juliusz Słowacki*
- *Little Zinnobers by Elena Chizhova*
- *We Are Building Capitalism! Moscow in Transition 1992-1997*
- *The Nuremberg Trials by Alexander Zvyagintsev*
- *The Hemingway Game by Evgeni Grishkovets*
- *A Flame Out at Sea by Dmitry Novikov*
- *Jesus' Cat by Grig*
- *Want a Baby and Other Plays by Sergei Tretyakov*
- *I Mikhail Bulgakov: The Life and Times by Marietta Chudakova*
- *Leonardo's Handwriting by Dina Rubina*